wondergirls™ 4th

Growing Pains

Jillian Brooks

SCHOLASTIC INC.
New York Toronto London Auckland Sydney
Mexico City New Delhi Hong Kong Buenos Aires

No part of this publication may be reproduced in whole or in part, or stored in a retrieval system or transmitted in any form by any means, electronic, mechanical, photocopying, recording, or otherwise, without written permission of the publisher. For information regarding permission, write to Scholastic Inc., Attention: Permissions Department, 557 Broadway, New York, NY 10012.

ISBN 0-439-45097-7

Produced by 17th Street Productions,
an Alloy, Inc. company
151 West 26th Street
New York, NY 10001

SCHOLASTIC and associated logos are trademarks and/or registered trademarks of Scholastic Inc.

12 11 10 9 8 7 6 5 4 3 2 1   3 4 5 6 7 8/0

Printed in the U.S.A.   40
First Scholastic printing, March 2003

chapter
ONE

Posted on the assignment board in art class

Attention: Anyone interested in extra credit (and fun!)
The art department needs your help! We have planned a school spirit mural for the exterior wall of the gym, and we need students to help paint. Anyone who helps with the mural will receive an extra A+ project factored into his or her final grade—and the undying gratitude of your art teacher!!

"Ugh! This looks ridiculous!" I moaned as I stepped back to survey my work. I was supposed to be painting a muskrat—our school mascot—on the back wall of the gym, but so far, it looked more like a dog . . . a very lumpy dog. Usually, I'm a pretty decent artist, but this was definitely not my best work. "What am I doing wrong?"

"Let me see, Amanda." Nandi Spencer, the vice president of the seventh grade, walked over and frowned at my muskrat. The school spirit mural had been Nandi's idea. I knew because I was president of the sixth grade, and I had been at the student government meeting when she brought it up. Not everyone had been wild about the idea, but Nandi had promised to organize everything herself. And she'd done it, too, with only a little help from the art department. "I don't think this is so bad," Nandi said, tugging thoughtfully on one of her braids. She dipped a paintbrush into some brown paint and went to work on the outline of my muskrat. It only took her about thirty seconds to even it out.

"That's so much better," I told her gratefully. "Now I can just fill it in. Thanks!"

"No problem," Nandi said with a grin. "I think this is really starting to come together!" Nandi was incredibly enthusiastic. Even though only four other people had shown up to help with the mural, she didn't act disappointed at all. I mean, *I* was disappointed. And surprised. After all, Mr. Tate, our art teacher, had even offered extra credit. Personally, I didn't need the extra points—I'd just come because I thought it would be fun. Besides, even though I didn't know Nandi well, I really liked the things she had to say in class council meetings. I wanted to help her with her project.

I watched as Nandi added a tree to the background. The branches and leaves were very realistic-looking, and the trunk seemed so solid that I almost felt like I could lean against it. In some ways, the tree in Nandi's picture looked better than the real trees that stood behind us. It was early December, and even though it was a pretty warm day—I was comfortable in a heavy sweater and my favorite embroidered jeans—the trees had already lost most of their leaves, and their bare branches looked bleak against the steel gray sky.

"So, Nandi," I said as I filled in my muskrat's body with brown paint, "do you take private art lessons?"

"No way," Nandi said wryly. "My parents think art is silly. They won't even buy me art supplies."

"What?" I asked. I couldn't believe it.

"It's true," Nandi said, frowning at the leaf she was painting. "They're both doctors, and they think that I should be focused on science. They want me to follow in their footsteps."

"But can't you be interested in art *and* science?" I asked.

"That's what I keep telling them." Nandi dipped her brush into some green paint and added another leaf to her tree. "But they won't listen. The only artistic thing I'm allowed to do is ballet because my dad is a serious fan."

I pressed my lips together and kept painting. Wow. I couldn't imagine what I would do if my parents wouldn't let me paint. Luckily, though, my dad and stepmom are way into art. And I have an awesome baby-sitter named Penny Zinsser who's an artist. (Actually, she's more like a friend since I'm really too old to have a baby-sitter. And now Penny baby-sits my little stepbrother and stepsister, Joey and Jessy.) Penny lives down the street from me and is always encouraging me to paint and sculpt. Her house is full of pieces she's made—mostly papier-mâché sculptures of imaginary creatures, like a purple hippopotamus or a blue walrus covered in stars.

"Hey, guys, how's it coming along?"

I turned to see one of my best friends, Felicia Fiol, walking toward us. Her long, curly dark hair bounced with every step. "Hey, Felicia!" I called. "Is it time for the game already?" Felicia and I had planned to watch the soccer game at four. Our other two best friends, Traci McClintic and Arielle Davis, are on the team. I couldn't wait. They were playing the Stanton Wolverines, Wonder Lake Middle School's biggest rivals.

"We've still got half an hour," Felicia said. "But Ms. McClintic let the orchestra go early so that everyone could get ready for the game." Traci's mom is the music teacher at our school and the orchestra director. "I thought I'd come over and help you guys with the mural, if you need me."

"Sure!" I said happily. "Do you know Nandi?"

Nandi smiled at Felicia. "Hi," she said. "If you want to paint part of the sky, that would be great."

4

"Okay," Felicia said. She found a paintbrush and dipped it in some blue paint.

"So—how are all of the animals?" I asked. Felicia's dad runs an animal shelter, and all four of us BFFs are volunteers. We even run a program called Healing Paws, where we bring some of the animals from the shelter to the children's ward of the Wonder Lake Hospital so the sick kids can have someone to play with.

"They're fine. I think they miss all of you guys," Felicia joked as she painted the sky with even strokes. "It's been two whole days since you've been over!"

"Tell them that we'll be over tomorrow," I said. "And that we miss them, too!"

Felicia laughed. "They'll be glad to hear it." She picked up the tub of blue paint and dipped in her brush as far as it would go. "You know," she said, "this is practically empty. There isn't enough to finish the sky."

"Nandi, is there more blue paint somewhere?" I asked.

Nandi shook her head. "That's all they gave us."

"Oh, well," I said, checking my watch. "It's almost time for the game, anyway. We should probably start cleaning up. We'll get some more paint from the art department next time."

I gathered everyone's brushes, and Nandi and Felicia collected the tubs of paint. We said good-bye to the other volunteers, then headed to the art room to clean up and put things away.

"Do you guys mind finishing up?" Nandi asked as she and Felicia put the paint tubs back into the cupboard. "My dad is picking me up for ballet class in three minutes."

"Go ahead," I told her. "All we have to do is rinse out the brushes." I let the water run over the bristles and watched as the colors faded, then disappeared down the drain.

"Thanks," Nandi said. The beads at the end of her braids clacked together as she flashed us a wide grin. "See you! It was great meeting you, Felicia."

"Same here," Felicia said warmly. "She seems really nice," Felicia whispered to me as soon as Nandi had disappeared through the door.

I nodded. Nandi really was great. I was glad that we'd been introduced through student council.

"Oh, hello, girls," Mr. Tate said as he walked into the classroom. "Cleaning up from the mural?"

"We just finished," I said as I dropped the last paintbrush handle-side-down into a jar to dry. "By the way, it looks like we're out of blue paint," I told him. "I thought I should let you know."

"Did you check the cupboard for more?" Mr. Tate asked.

"There isn't any," Felicia said. "I just looked."

Mr. Tate ran a hand through his curly brown hair

and sighed. "Oh, shoot," he said. "I don't know what to do."

"What do you mean?" I asked.

"I've been paying for these art supplies myself," Mr. Tate explained. "But I can't afford to keep doing it. Paint is much more expensive than you'd think."

"I know," I said. Penny had told me the same thing many times. "But won't the school pay you back?"

Mr. Tate frowned. "The art budget has been slashed. The money they gave me for supplies only lasted for the first six weeks of school. When I explained the situation at the last board meeting, they told me not to bother asking for more." Mr. Tate shook his head and sighed. "And now it looks like the budget is about to get slashed again at the meeting next week."

"That's terrible!" Felicia said.

"But how can they expect you to teach art classes without supplies?" I asked.

Mr. Tate shrugged. "I really don't know the answer to that, Amanda."

I couldn't believe it. An image of Nandi popped into my mind. The only training in art she got was in school. I wondered whether she would be able to take art classes at all next year. Maybe not, if there was no money for supplies. And what did this mean for the mural project? Would we even be able to finish it?

"This mural project is costing more than I thought it would," Mr. Tate went on. "Do you think that you could take up a collection from the kids who are volunteering to buy more paint?"

I had opened my mouth to say that was a great idea when I noticed that Felicia was staring at her shoes. My stomach sank. Of course—Felicia's dad ran an animal shelter, and her mom owned a bakery. Neither one of them made much money. They couldn't afford to fund a mural project any more than Mr. Tate could. And who knew how many of the other kids who had volunteered were in the same boat? I felt a sudden flash of anger. "It's just not fair," I said. "The school board has the money—why do they expect the teachers and students to fund the arts program ourselves?"

"Yeah," Felicia agreed. "They just gave the volleyball team money for new equipment. Why can't they give you money for paint?"

"I agree with you," Mr. Tate said, "but there isn't much I can do about it."

I twirled a piece of my long brown hair around my finger, thinking. "Wait," I said, "nothing is official until the school board votes on the funding next week, right?"

"But the members have already said that they plan to vote in favor of funding the athletics department," Mr. Tate said.

"That's okay," I said happily. "All we have to do is change their minds!"

Felicia smiled at me. "And just how are we going to do that?" she asked.

"Well, I'd already planned on saying a few words at the school board meeting," I admitted. I'd known for a while now that the arts budget could get cut, and I'd always planned on saying something about it. "But that was before I realized just how bad the situation was. Now it looks like I'll have to come up with some sort of full-blown presentation," I said. "Graphs, charts—you name it. We've got to show those guys that arts education is seriously important." I hoped that my voice sounded confident, but my stomach was doing flip-flops big time. I hate speaking in public. Just the idea of standing up and telling the school board my *name* makes me feel weak in the knees—and here I was, saying that I was going to persuade them to change the entire budget? Still, I felt like I couldn't just stand by and let the school board slash arts funding to zero.

"Well, I wish you good luck," Mr. Tate said. "You're going to need it, believe me."

I swallowed hard and looked at Felicia, who smiled. "You can do it, Amanda," she said encouragingly. "And I'll help."

The stiff knot in my stomach loosened a little. "Thanks, Felicia." Felicia is a really great friend. She can be kind of shy sometimes, but I can almost always count on her to back me up when I need it. Sometimes she seems to believe in Arielle, Traci, and me more than she believes in herself.

I whipped out a small notebook and made some notes on what I wanted to say to the school board. Getting organized always helps me conquer my nerves. "Okay," I said, "the first thing I need to do is talk to the student council. We'll be in a much better position if the entire student government agrees that the arts funding shouldn't be cut. And maybe Asher Bank will want to make the presentation himself," I added hopefully. Asher Bank is the president of the student body and the eighth grader who had persuaded me to run for student government in the first place. He's well known and liked among the faculty and staff as well as the students. If he made the speech, the school board would definitely listen.

"Great idea," Felicia said. "So the first step is to make a strong presentation for the student council."

"I have some information on how arts education can improve learning in other subjects," Mr. Tate said. "I can bring it to you tomorrow."

"That would be great," I said, jotting everything down in the notebook as quickly as I could. "The student council is meeting tomorrow afternoon. I can look over the information during lunch."

"Okay," Mr. Tate said. "You can meet me here before school." The corners of his eyes crinkled into a hopeful smile, and I felt a little better. Maybe we really did have a chance at changing the school board's mind.

Felicia and I thanked Mr. Tate and walked out into

the hall. It was only a few minutes before four—the soccer game was about to start. Felicia was saying something about Traci and Arielle, but I couldn't concentrate on her words. My mind was still whirling with ideas about the speech I was going to have to make before the student council. *This has to work*, I thought. *It just has to.* I had to get the student council on my side. After all, I had been elected class president because I had promised that I wouldn't let the school board cut the arts budget. Well, sort of. I had made that promise, and I had been elected class president. But that was really only because Arielle had backed out of the election at the last minute, and I had been the only candidate left. Still, I knew that people would be expecting me to take a stand when it came time for the school board's vote. I wasn't about to back down now.

I wouldn't let the arts budget disappear without a fight. And with the rest of the student council behind me, I knew that we could make the school board change its mind. I just knew it.

chapter
TWO

Come see the Wonder Lake
Middle School Muskrats
take on our rivals,
the Stanton Wolverines!!
Game time: 4:00 p.m.
Don't miss the match of the millennium!!
Gooooooooooooooal!

"Hurry!" Felicia said as we neared the soccer field. "They've already started."

"I didn't realize that Traci was playing today," I said, spotting our friend's familiar blond ponytail on the field. Arielle was there, too, her auburn hair tied into a smooth French braid. Arielle always managed to look perfect—even in her blue-and-white soccer uniform. She was dribbling the ball intently, dodging this way and that, trying to lose the giant from Stanton who was hot on her heels. Arielle had been my best friend since we were in pre-K, and she was the star of the soccer team. Traci had just moved to town this year from South Carolina. She was a really good soccer player, too, but she didn't play in as many games as Arielle did.

"Carly Michaels sprained her ankle," Felicia explained as we jogged toward the crowded bleachers set up at the sidelines. "So Traci's in for the next couple of weeks."

A huge cheer went up from the bleachers as Arielle made a shot on goal. But the cheer quickly turned to a groan as one of the tall Stanton girls headed the ball away from the net.

Felicia and I stood at the edge of the bleachers for a moment, looking for seats. There weren't any. "Maybe we should just stand by the sidelines," I suggested.

"Good idea," Felicia agreed. "Look, there's Ryan."

"Go, Muskrats!" Ryan Bradley shouted as we joined him. "Show those Wolverines that you aren't just cute and cuddly!" I laughed. Ryan would have been the sixth grade's official class clown—if those things were ever official.

All of the girls on the field ignored him. They were focused on the game. A moment later there was a groan from the stands as one of the Wolverines kicked the ball into the net over our goalie's head.

"Yikes," Felicia said. "This is not looking good."

"Is it just me," Ryan asked, "or do those Stanton girls look like they've been taking way too many vitamins?"

"They are kind of tall," I admitted. In fact, the

Stanton players towered over our Wonder Lake team. They were also wearing crisp red-and-black uniforms with a picture of a fierce-looking wolverine on the front. Personally, I'd never seen a picture of a wolverine before. I have to say that it looked like something I didn't ever want to see in person. "I like their uniforms," I said.

"They're new," Felicia said.

"Unlike ours," Ryan put in. It was true. Next to the Stanton team, our team's blue-and-white uniforms looked tired and dingy. Even though we had a bunch of excellent players, Stanton made the Wonder Lake team look like a bunch of kids who had accidentally ended up in a matchup against a team from women's major-league soccer.

"Let's go, Arielle!" I shouted, figuring that our team needed a little encouragement.

"You can do it, Traci!" Felicia joined in.

"Come on, Traci!" Ryan said, clapping like crazy. "Kick us a go-*wal*!"

Traci shot Ryan an irritated look. She had a slight Southern accent, and Ryan liked to tease her about it. But even though Ryan sometimes got on Traci's nerves, I knew that she still liked him. A lot. And I knew that Ryan wouldn't bother teasing Traci if he didn't like her, too. They weren't officially a "couple," but I was sort of starting to think of them that way.

"I can't believe how many people showed up for

the game," I said, shading my eyes and looking up at the stands. It looked like the entire school was packed into the bleachers.

"We haven't won against Stanton in eight years," Ryan said.

"Wow," Felicia said. Her brown eyes were wide. She turned back toward the field and yelled, "Come on, Arielle and Traci!"

A Stanton player with short brown hair tried to pass the ball to one of her teammates, but Arielle stole it at the last second and darted back toward the opposite end of the field. She took off before any of the Stanton players had a chance to catch her. In a flash she had reached the goal and slammed the ball into the net. The score was tied!

"Way to go!" I screamed. Felicia was jumping up and down, shouting, and Ryan pumped his fist in the air. Arielle grinned as Traci ran over and gave her a hug.

"That was great," Felicia said as the players headed back to the bench to huddle up. It was halftime.

"Our team is good, but our halftime is lame," Ryan said. "Where's the entertainment? Where's the snacks?"

People had gotten up from the stands and were milling around, chatting and stretching their legs.

"We've never had snacks at these events," I said. "I think the school is convinced that the field would end up covered in napkins."

"Someone should tell them to try it out," Ryan said. "They could make a ton of money! I, for one, am totally starved, and I bet half of these people are, too."

"I could go for some hot chocolate," Felicia agreed, blowing on her hands as a cool breeze lifted her hair off her face.

"Did someone say hot chocolate?" asked a voice behind me.

I turned to see Dave McClintic smiling at us, and my heart did a little flutter. Traci's brother is an eighth grader and supernice—not to mention cute. His light blond hair was tousled from the wind, and his freckles had faded into his skin, which had gone slightly pink in the cool air. "Tell me that they're selling hot chocolate somewhere," he said. "I'd buy five cups of it."

"See?" Ryan said to me. "The school would be rich."

I rolled my eyes at him. "Hi, Dave," I said. "Want to join us?"

"Sure," he said, his smile widening. When I'd first met Dave, he had been kind of shy and tongue-tied. But we'd been hanging together more lately, and now that I knew him better, he seemed to have gotten over his shyness. Maybe he just needed time to get used to Wonder Lake and all. "I just got here," Dave went on. "What's the score?"

"One to one," Felicia said. "And it looks like they're starting again."

Our team broke their huddle with a clap and ran out to join the Stanton players on the field. Traci frowned slightly as she sized up the girl she was guarding. She looked completely focused.

The whistle blew, and Arielle took off with the ball, squirting it through her opponent's legs and picking up the dribble on the other side. Traci followed Arielle downfield, the girl who was guarding Traci right behind her.

Ryan let loose with a cheer. "One, two, three, *four*, kick the goal we're waiting *for!* Go-o-o-o-o-o-o, Traci!"

Traci shot him another annoyed glance. But in the next moment she turned her attention back to Arielle, who was having trouble getting past the tall African-American girl who was guarding her. Arielle passed the ball to Traci.

Dave laughed at Ryan's cheer. "Yeah, Traci!" he yelled. "One, two, three, four, steal the ball and make the *score!*"

Traci's eyes flickered to Dave quickly and seemed to register surprise at seeing him standing with us. But she turned her focus back to the game almost immediately. Traci dribbled a few steps downfield, but there was no way she could make it past her guard. She passed it right back to Arielle.

"Or we'll kick you out the *door!*" Ryan added.

Felicia and I looked at each other and giggled. We couldn't help it—the cheers were just too goofy. Dave glanced at me and smiled, and my heart did that little fluttery thing again.

Traci glared at the guys, who cracked up. Arielle dribbled back upfield for a few steps, and Traci took the opportunity to fake out her opponent. Just then Arielle made her move, shooting a pass to Traci. The ball moved so fast, it was nothing but a blur as Traci lined up her shot.

"Make a shot that we'll *adore!*" Ryan screeched.

Traci kicked the ball wide. The crowd groaned as it rolled harmlessly away from the goal. Traci planted her hands on her hips and shook her head, clearly angry with herself. Arielle frowned.

Ryan improvised another cheer. "That's okay, please don't pout! You will beat them, there's no *doubt!*"

"The Wolverines will still *wipe out!*" Dave added.

Ryan slapped him five and put in, "You'll turn them into *sauerkraut!*"

"Hey, guys, I think we'd better cool it," Felicia said gently, casting a glance toward the field.

I looked over and saw that Traci was glaring in our direction. She looked at me, then looked at Dave and scowled. I gulped. This was not good. Sometimes it felt a little awkward to have a crush on the brother of one of my absolute best friends. Even though Dave and I had been hanging out more lately, we hadn't really been together much when Traci was around. I definitely didn't want Traci to think that I was choosing Dave over her or something. "You know, I think Felicia's right," I said.

Dave grimaced as he caught the tail end of Traci's look. "I guess we did kind of break her concentration," he admitted sheepishly.

"Yeah," Ryan agreed. He looked kind of embarrassed.

Traci squinted and turned her attention back to the game as Dave, Ryan, Felicia, and I clapped and shouted her name. No one made up a cheer, though.

The Stanton goalie kicked the ball back into play, and the African-American girl streaked toward it. I hardly had time to blink before she rocketed it into our goal.

"Ugh!" Felicia said. "Now it's two to one. And there's hardly any time left."

"We can still come back," Ryan said. His voice was confident, but his face had gone pale, and I could tell that he was feeling guilty for distracting Traci earlier.

"Come on, Traci," Dave murmured. His hands were clenched into fists. "You can do it."

The Stanton girl with short dark hair was dribbling the ball toward our goal, but Arielle swooped in and stole it, sprinting downfield. The tall African-American girl thundered after her.

"Over here!" Traci shouted. She was wide open!

Arielle ignored her. She grimaced and pulled her

leg back to score, but the angle was a tough one. Arielle kicked the shot, but the Stanton goalie leaped toward it. She put a hand on it, and the ball hit the crossbar and bounced away.

The game was over—we had lost.

All of the Wonder Lake players came over to pat Arielle on the back . . . well, almost all of them. I noticed Traci was still standing on the field, rooted to her spot, as though she couldn't believe that Arielle hadn't passed the ball to her. Personally, I couldn't believe it, either. I shook my head.

"She should have passed it," Felicia said quietly. I looked at her. It wasn't like Felicia to criticize any-one—especially Arielle. But Felicia was totally right.

It looked like we were in for some fireworks between Arielle and Traci. And it looked like Wonder Lake would *never* beat Stanton. I sighed. This day was turning into a serious bummer.

chapter
THREE

Instant Messages from FiFiol to FlowerGrl

```
    FiFiol:  R u there?
 FlowerGrl:  Barely :o{
    FiFiol:  Still working on ur presentation
             for class council?
 FlowerGrl:  Yep. I'm so nervous!
    FiFiol:  Don't worry—u'll do great!!
 FlowerGrl:  Thanx. If council doesn't go along
             with this, I don't know what
             I'll do. . . .
    FiFiol:  They'll back u. They have 2!
```

Felicia and Arielle were already sitting at our usual table by the window when I walked into the cafeteria the next day. I hurried to join them, my fingers wrapped tightly around the manila folder I was carrying. In it were the notes that Mr. Tate had given me before school. I wanted to look them over as soon as possible.

"Hey!" Felicia smiled when she saw me. "Where's your lunch tray?"

21

I held up a brown paper bag as I slid into the seat next to Arielle. "I brought a sandwich. Actually, I have to run over to the library for the rest of lunch. I just wanted to come by and say hi." I turned to Arielle. "That was an exciting game yesterday," I told her. "You played well."

"Not that it helped much." Arielle frowned and fiddled with the fish sticks on her tray.

"You'll beat them next time," Felicia said, touching Arielle's elbow gently.

Arielle shrugged and gave her smooth auburn hair an impatient flip. "Maybe." She dipped a Tater Tot into ketchup and took a bite. "Ugh, why do I eat these?" she asked as she quickly spat it back into her napkin. "I always think they're going to be good, and they're always disgusting."

"Hey, guys," Traci said as she slid her tray onto the table and sat down across from Felicia.

"Hi," I said. I was about to congratulate Traci on the game, too, but then I noticed that Traci was looking at Arielle uneasily. Arielle was frowning at her Tater Tots as if they had committed a crime. Suddenly, soccer seemed like an unsafe topic. I racked my brain for something to say, but I came up totally dry.

"So," Felicia said brightly, "you guys are coming over later, right? The puppies are getting bigger, and they are *so* cute." I smiled at her. Felicia always hated it when we fought, and I guessed she could sense the tension between Arielle and Traci as well as I could.

"I can't wait to see them," Traci said. The mixed-breed puppies had been born about a month ago, and they were seriously adorable. The last time we'd gone to the animal shelter, we spent half the time playing with the puppies and nearly forgot to feed the cats until Mr. Fiol reminded us.

"Oh yeah, I can't wait," Arielle echoed in a voice that seemed barely interested. Still, I could tell that there was a small smile curling at the corners of her lips and eyes. She wasn't wild about animals, but I knew that she had a soft spot for the puppies.

"I'll have to meet you guys there," I said. "I have a student council meeting."

Just then a Tater Tot sailed over our table and landed in Traci's water glass with a tiny splash.

We all turned to look in the direction that the Tater Tot had come from and saw Ryan waving frantically, a goofy grin on his face.

"Was he aiming for the water glass?" Felicia asked. "If so, that was a pretty good shot."

"Ryan is so immature," Arielle growled. "He'd better not throw any food near my new outfit." Arielle was wearing a crisp white shirt. I could only imagine what she would do if it ended up with ketchup smeared across it.

I shrugged. "He can be pretty funny sometimes," I said. I looked over at Traci, expecting her to defend

Ryan. But she didn't say anything. She just kept staring at her water glass. The water magnified the Tater Tot, making it appear enormous.

"Like once or twice a year," Arielle countered.

"Yeah," Traci agreed. "He thinks he's hilarious—but he can be a real pain." She stood up. "I'm going to get some more water," she announced. She didn't even glance in Ryan's direction as she walked away.

I looked over at Ryan and saw his grin die away. He pressed his lips together, then shrugged and turned back to his friends. I felt bad for him, but I understood where Traci was coming from. She was still mad about the way Ryan had distracted her yesterday. Still, I knew he hadn't meant to mess up her game. And I figured that Traci knew it, too. She just needed some time to snap out of her postgame funk.

I stood up just as Traci came back with some fresh water. "I've got to get to the library," I said.

"Working on your student council presentation?" Felicia asked.

I nodded. "I'll let you all know how it goes," I promised as I gave them a little wave and headed for the exit.

"Good luck," Arielle called after me.

I thought that was pretty sweet of Arielle, considering that I hadn't even had a chance to tell her what the presentation was about. I grinned and gave her a thumbs-up, but the truth was that I didn't feel confident at all. On my way out the door I threw my sandwich in the garbage. I was way too nervous to eat it.

Thank goodness Mr. Tate gave me all of these notes, I thought as I hurried toward the library. *Maybe I can let the facts do the talking.*

The minute the final bell rang, I dashed to room 246, where the student council meetings were held. Of course, I was the first person there, so I sat down and flipped through my notes as people filed into the classroom. This was one of the bigger classrooms, and the teacher had arranged the chairs in a circle so that everyone could see one another. In some ways it was a good thing, and in some ways it was a bad thing. I knew everyone would be able to hear me, but when I thought about people looking at me as I gave my speech . . . ugh. Shivers.

After a few minutes people began shuffling in, talking and laughing. I buried my nose in my notes. I didn't want to forget anything once I started speaking.

"Amanda," Nandi said as she slid into the desk next to mine, "I spoke to Mr. Tate this morning, and he told me all about the funding cuts—I can't believe it." Her brown eyes were wide. "We *have* to do something."

"We will." I nodded at my notes. "I'm going to bring it up at the meeting."

"Great," Nandi said. "The whole student council should work together on this."

"Is everyone here?" Asher Bank, an eighth grader and president of the student council, asked a moment later. He was leaning casually against the teacher's desk as he looked around the room, and I smiled at the confidence in his voice. It was easy to picture him making a speech to the school board. *I bet he could even get them to* increase *the arts budget*, I thought as Asher went on. "Okay, let's get started. Our first item is the annual candy sale—"

I waited patiently as he ran through the agenda items, but I could hardly concentrate on what he was saying. All I cared about was the arts budget. But it wasn't on the official agenda, so I couldn't bring it up until the end. Finally, Asher got through his report on the recommendation to revise the school dress code and asked if there was any new business.

My hand shot into the air. "I have something," I said, without waiting to be recognized.

Asher lifted his eyebrows at me, clearly surprised. I didn't usually speak much during student council meetings. "Yes, Amanda?" he said.

I cleared my throat, suddenly shy, and glanced down at my notes. "Um . . . the school board is meeting next week, and I've heard that they're planning to cut the arts budget. By a lot." I looked up. Everyone was staring at me. I glanced at Nandi, who nodded encouragingly. I forced myself to go on. "They, um, they want to spend the money on the athletics department instead, which I think is totally unfair. I have some, uh, studies"—I flipped through my notes—"that show an arts education helps with student self-esteem and even improves mental skills. . . ." Oh, no. I couldn't find the page that I was looking for. Suddenly, my mind went blank—I couldn't think of what to say next. I felt my face grow hot. I wanted to hide behind my notes. Ugh! This was why I didn't want to speak to the school board!

"If we let them cut the arts budget, who knows what they'll cut next?" Nandi put in. "Besides, there are students in this school who want to have a career in the arts."

I smiled at her gratefully and gave up looking for my page. I'd just have to wing it from here. "Right," I said. "When I ran for president of the sixth grade, I promised that I wouldn't let the school board cut arts funding. Now, I think we should go to the school board meeting and let them know that the student council is against the cuts." I looked around the room. I saw Peter Silver cast a sideways glance at Cassandra Jackson, who frowned. *What's that about?* I wondered. Cassandra was president of the seventh grade, and Peter was treasurer.

"Hmmm," Asher said. He ran a hand through his curly dark hair and cast his dark eyes around the circle. "Does anyone else have anything to say about this?"

"Well," Cassandra said slowly, "I do." She turned

her large black eyes on me. "The problem is that the only way to fund the arts program is to cut money from sports since the school board can't afford increased funding for both. And when I ran for class president, I promised that I would work to get our teams new equipment." She looked around the room. "I think that we can all agree that the Wonder Lake sports teams have got some seriously ugly uniforms." A ripple of agreement ran through the class council. "I'm sorry," Cassandra went on, "but I just can't agree that we should fund arts over sports."

"I agree," Peter chimed in. "Sports are important. If people want art classes, let them take private lessons."

I felt like someone had punched me in the stomach. How could they be saying these things? Was I the only person who thought that the arts were important?

"Should we take a vote?" Asher said.

No, I wanted to scream. *No—wait—I haven't convinced you yet!* I opened my mouth to speak, but no words came out.

"Let's have a show of hands," Asher went on. "All those in favor of funding arts?"

I raised my hand as high as it would go. Nandi did, too. But we were the only ones.

"All those in favor of funding sports?" Asher asked.

The room blurred, but even through my tears I could see that everyone's hand was raised. I blinked hard. I hated to cry. It was so embarrassing. I wished that a hole would open in the floor and swallow me up.

"I'm sorry, Amanda," Asher said. "But we clearly can't support your proposal. In fact," he went on, looking around the room, "I think we should formally oppose it."

"I second the motion," Cassandra said. Then there was another vote, and everyone but Nandi and me agreed to recommend diverting money from the arts budget to the sports teams.

I looked at Nandi, who bit her lip. Oh, no. This was the worst possible thing that could have happened. Now Asher would definitely be giving a speech in front of the school board. But he would be saying all the wrong things!

"What should we do now?" Nandi whispered as Asher announced that the meeting was over. Everyone started milling around, gathering books, and filing out of the room.

"I don't know," I admitted. "But I don't want to give up."

"Me either," Nandi agreed.

"Amanda," said a voice behind me. It was Asher. "Listen, I'm sorry about what happened at the meeting," he said, his brown eyes sympathetic. "I know that wasn't what you were hoping for."

I shrugged. Asher was trying to be nice, but I didn't know what to say.

"I think that you should go to the school board meeting and tell them what you told us," Asher went on. "Hey, at the very least the school board will see that the students are worried about both departments—there's always the chance that they'll increase the budget overall."

Easy for you to say, I thought. *You aren't deathly terrified of public speaking.* But I didn't say any of that to Asher. Instead I just smiled at him, but it felt forced. "I'll think about it," I told him.

"I think he's right," Nandi said as Asher walked away. "Listen, we have to give it a try, right?"

I sighed, picturing myself standing before the school board. My heart started pounding like crazy at the thought—especially after what had just happened at the meeting. But I knew that Nandi and Asher were right. I couldn't just stand by and let this happen. "Right," I said finally.

"Good." Nandi smiled. "You can count on me."

"Thanks, Nandi," I said, grateful that I would have her help. I knew one thing for sure—I was going to need it.

chapter
FOUR

From the desk of Luis Fiol

Hi, girls!

I had to run and pick up some puppy food and run a few other errands—be back in an hour or so. In the meantime would you please clean out the kennels, feed the cats and ferrets, and give the puppies a bath? We want them to smell sweet for their next Healing Paws outing!

"No! Stop!" Arielle cried as I hurried around the side of Felicia's dad's house to the animal shelter. She had been hosing down a wiggly black puppy, who had decided to give himself a good shake—spraying water everywhere.

Arielle let go of the puppy and held up her hands to shield her face from the water. The puppy took the golden opportunity to dash off . . . into a mud puddle.

Traci cracked up, and I was glad that she seemed to be over the post-soccer-game funk she'd been in at lunch. "You're supposed to make them cleaner, not dirtier, Arielle," Traci said. She and Felicia were soaping another puppy in a metal washtub. It was so covered in suds, I couldn't even tell what kind of dog it was.

"Ha-ha," Arielle said. "I don't suppose anyone wants to help me catch this mutt. I don't want to get mud on my new shirt—or my platform sneakers." I grinned. We'd all put on heavy aprons before we started bathing the puppies, but they weren't doing much to protect against these kinds of shenanigans. The black puppy let out a happy yelp and rolled on his back playfully. Arielle rolled her eyes, but she couldn't hide her smile. The puppy's name was Buster, and he was the absolute favorite of one of the girls we visited in the hospital with Healing Paws. I knew that Arielle thought Buster was pretty cute, too.

"I'll help you," I volunteered.

"Oh, hey, Amanda!" Felicia said. "How did the student council meeting go?"

"Don't ask," I said as I dropped my book bag and scooped up the muddy puppy. Buster squirmed and tried to lick me, but I was careful to hold him away from my clothes. I carried him over to Traci, who put him back into the washtub for a second sudsing.

"What happened?" Arielle asked as she took the other puppy, a black-and-white mix named Swirl, and began hosing off her suds. "Were you making some kind of speech or something?"

I sighed. "The school board wants to cut the arts budget and add to the sports budget," I explained. "They're voting next week, and I was hoping that the student council would help me stop them."

"But they didn't agree?" Felicia asked, frowning.

I shook my head and grabbed a towel. "Nope. In fact, they voted to recommend cutting the arts budget." I started patting Swirl with the towel. She looked up at me with big, patient eyes.

"That's awful!" Felicia cried.

"Whatever," Arielle snapped as she started hosing down Buster—again. "Personally, I think they *should* cut the arts budget. All of the teachers in that department are total cornflakes."

"Hey!" Traci said, flushing red with anger. "My mom works in that department!"

"Point made," Arielle muttered under her breath, then said, "Sorry," in a voice loud enough for Traci to hear.

Traci didn't say anything else, but I could see her jaw muscles working, as if she was gritting her teeth. I knew it wasn't easy for Traci to have a mom who worked at the school. And the truth was, Ms. McClintic *could* be a little spacey. But she was really nice. And I'd heard that she was actually a pretty tough music teacher. I knew for a fact that the orchestra sounded better than it had in years.

"Look, the arts are really important, and they need the money—" I began.

"Oh, please," Arielle cut me off. "I'm with the rest of the student council on this one, Amanda. I mean, look at our soccer uniforms! They're, like, ten years old! The sports teams need the money *way* more than the arts department does."

"That's totally not true!" I said hotly. I couldn't believe Arielle wasn't backing me up on this! How would she like it if she found out that the school was cutting the soccer budget? "Look, at least you guys *have* uniforms," I said, "unlike the arts department, which can't even afford paint."

"It would be better if we *didn't* have uniforms," Arielle countered. "Then maybe we could buy our own. The ones we have make us look like serious nerds."

"How can you say that?" I demanded. I turned to Felicia and Traci. "You guys, back me up." I put Swirl into a dog carrier and began to gently rub Buster dry.

"I totally agree with you," Felicia said. "Sorry, Arielle," she added quickly.

Traci shrugged. "Well, I don't know," she admitted. "I kind of think Arielle has a point."

I gaped at her. "You do?" I asked.

Traci looked at Arielle, then at me. "Yeah. I mean, new uniforms aren't just about fashion," she said. "They can give a team a psychological advantage. Look at Stanton. You can't help thinking, 'Oh, wow, this is a serious team,' when you see their uniforms."

"Especially because all of their players wear a size extra large," Arielle added dryly.

I bit my lip. I hadn't thought of it that way. Traci had a good point, although I still thought that it was important to keep the arts budget from being cut.

"And I really think that the school as a whole gets more from sports than from arts," Traci added.

"Traci, how can you say that?" Felicia demanded. "Do you want the orchestra funds to get cut?"

Traci blushed. "No," she said quickly.

"Because that's what's going to happen," Felicia said. "It's sports or arts—one or the other."

Traci sighed. "I guess soccer is just more important to me than orchestra," she admitted finally. "I'm sorry." She really did sound sorry as she said it, and she ducked her head guiltily. I guessed she was thinking about her mom. The truth was, if the budget got cut, Ms. McClintic might not have a job next year— or she might only have a part-time job. At the very least the orchestra wouldn't be going on any more trips like the recent one they had taken to Chicago for a competition.

"Well, I'm sorry, too," Felicia snapped. "Orchestra is important to me, and so is the arts budget in general. And I don't think it should be cut just so that you guys can look good on the soccer field. What matters is how you *play*." She stood up and dragged the washtub over to some hedges, then dumped the water over the roots. I had to smile a little. Felicia didn't usually get mad. In fact, she hated fighting. I was glad that she felt strongly enough about the arts budget to say something about it to Traci and Arielle.

"We'll play better if we have new uniforms," Arielle said flippantly. "Believe me."

"Okay," Felicia said. Then she turned to me. "So—what does all of this mean? Are you still going to say something to the school board?"

"Definitely," I said. "And Nandi is going to help me."

"I'm in, too," Felicia said quickly. "Just let me know what I can do to help."

"Thanks, Felicia." I grinned at her a moment. But when I looked at Traci and Arielle, my grin faltered a little. Both of them were looking at their shoes. They weren't going to help me. I don't know why it surprised me, but it did. Somehow I'd kind of thought that they would back me even if they disagreed with me.

Just then there was the sound of gravel crunching on the driveway as Penny's car pulled up. I checked my watch. Wow! I hadn't realized that it was so late already. Penny was here to pick me up.

"Hi, girls," Penny said as she stepped out of the car.

Everyone chorused hello as Penny peered around, looking a little nervous. "Is the coast clear?" she asked. Penny used to be seriously afraid of all dogs. Lately, she'd been coming with us on our Healing Paws trips, and she was getting used to the smaller, gentler ones. But the big ones still freaked her out—especially if they were running right toward her.

"Totally clear," I said quickly. "Do you want to see some very cute, nonscary puppies?"

Penny laughed. "I think I can handle that," she said.

I pulled Buster out of the dog carrier and handed him to Penny. He was very fluffy and wiggled in her hands as she held him awkwardly.

"He won't bite you," Traci said. "But he might try to lick you to death."

Penny giggled as Buster licked her hand. "I see what you mean," she said. "Hi, Felicia. Is your dad here?"

"He's running errands," Felicia said quickly. "But I'll let him know that you were here." Her arms were folded across her chest, and she was frowning slightly.

"Okeydokey," Penny said. "I'll just give him a call later. Sorry, little fella, it's time for me to take Amanda home." Penny was looking at Buster when she said that, so she didn't see Felicia roll her eyes. But I did. I sighed. I wished that Felicia liked Penny a little more. We both felt weird because Penny was dating her dad. In fact, Felicia and I had tried to break them up once a few months ago. We'd gotten into major trouble for it, too. And just a couple of weeks ago, around Felicia's birthday, we became convinced that Penny and Mr. Fiol were breaking up, and we sort of tried to get him back together with Felicia's mom—unsuccessfully. But now I was getting used to the idea of Penny dating Mr. Fiol, though I still thought they made a pretty strange couple. I mean, Mr. Fiol ran an animal shelter, and Penny had always been afraid of dogs! "We'd better get going," Penny said to me. "Adele told me that dinner would be ready at six." Adele is my stepmom.

"Okay," I said. "Bye, you guys."

"Bye," Felicia said.

Traci waved. "See you tomorrow."

Arielle just shrugged and flipped her hair over her shoulder. Obviously, she was mad at me. Oh, well. I couldn't worry about it. I had other things on my mind. Besides, I knew that Arielle would get over it. She always did.

I climbed into Penny's car and waved to my friends as she backed out of the driveway. I stared at the trees that whizzed by the car window as Penny drove me home, thinking about my best friends. I just hoped that Felicia wouldn't change her mind about helping me and Nandi with the school board presentation. I knew how much Felicia liked to keep the peace among us. *Then again, she might* not *change her mind*, I thought, remembering the expression on Felicia's face as she'd talked about how important orchestra was to her. I really hoped she wouldn't. I mean, I was glad that Nandi was going to help me and all. But the people I really needed were my friends. And I felt better knowing that at least one of them would be with me when I spoke to the school board.

Well, I felt a *little* better. But a little better would have to be good enough.

chapter
FIVE

Instant Messages from FiFio1 to PrincessA

    FiFio1: Hi. Didn't c u at lunch.
PrincessA: Had to run. Needed to study for
                Spanish quiz. Muy difícil!
    FiFio1: Amanda sez u guys had a fight.
PrincessA: Moi? ;o)
    FiFio1: Then everything's okay?
PrincessA: Don't worry about it. It'll blow
                over as soon as Amanda apologizes.
    FiFio1: What if she doesn't?
PrincessA: She will. She always does when she
                realizes that I'm right.

"Traci!" I called.

Traci didn't hear me. She was too busy trying to cram her math book into her locker, which was already overflowing with books and papers. Traci could be pretty organized, but she wasn't exactly the queen of neat.

"Traci," I said again, just as she managed to slam

her locker shut before anything tumbled out of it. I shuddered to think what would happen when she opened it again.

"Oh, hi!" Traci said with a smile. "Heading to lunch?"

I nodded. "Do you have a test?" I asked, pointing at the social studies book that she still held in her hand.

"Ugh, yes," Traci said. "I heard that there's a pop quiz today, so I thought I should look over the chapter at lunch. Besides," she added with a grin, "it's easier than shoving it into my locker."

I laughed, glad that Traci was in a better mood today. "No wonder you're such a good student," I said.

"Yeah," Traci agreed. "My bad habits come in handy sometimes."

I hugged my binder against my chest. I almost said something about how I had to work during lunch, too, because I wanted to look over the cost of funding the visual arts in our school. But I rejected the idea. "I can't wait for Healing Paws on Saturday," I said instead. The night before, I had decided not to bring up the arts budget with her or Arielle again. After all, I understood where they were coming from—they just had different priorities. There was no point in arguing about it. We would just have to agree to disagree.

"Same here," Traci said warmly.

I smiled at her. See? All we had to do was talk

about things we had in common, and our differences would work themselves out.

"Hey, Traci. Hey, Amanda," a familiar voice behind me said.

I turned and found myself looking directly into Dave's large brown eyes. He smiled at me and jammed his hands in his pockets. I felt myself blush slightly.

"Hi, Dave," I said. "We were just about to head to lunch. Want to join us?" I didn't even think about what I was saying, and the minute the words were out of my mouth, I realized my mistake. Dave smiled, but Traci's eyes clouded over.

Dave opened his mouth to reply, then glanced at his sister and seemed to change his mind. "Thanks for the offer, Amanda," he said, "but I already told some friends that I'd sit with them. Actually, I just came over to give you this." He handed a note to Traci. "It's from Mom," he explained.

Traci unfolded the note and skimmed it quickly. "She wants me to help her run a few errands after school," Traci explained. "And she says that *you* should only have two cookies when you get home, not the whole box," she said to Dave.

Dave rolled his eyes. "She already told me that."

I laughed, and Dave smiled at me. "That's a mom's job, I guess," I said.

"I think our mom is a little too into being the cookie police," Dave said.

"Okay, Dave, thanks for dropping this off," Traci said quickly.

"Oh, no problem," Dave said. He was still smiling at me. I sneaked a sideways peek at Traci and saw that she was frowning.

"Dave," Traci snapped, "you can *go* now."

Dave's eyebrows flew up, and his face turned pink. I could see how embarrassed he felt, and my heart sank. "Oh, right," he said quickly. "Uh—okay. Well . . . I guess I'll see you guys later." He turned and hurried down the hall.

I had to bite my lip to keep from saying anything to Traci as she and I fell into step toward the cafeteria. I mean, I understood that—to her—Dave was just an annoying older brother. But she knew that *I* thought he was really nice and cute. Traci had never had a problem with me liking Dave before. . . . Then again, I'd never invited him to sit with us before. I guess she just didn't want him hanging around. I wanted to tell Traci that I thought she hadn't been very nice to him, but I realized it wasn't really any of my business. Still—I felt bad for Dave. I just wished there was some way I could make Dave feel less awkward around us. . . . "You know what?" I said suddenly. "I just realized that I left something in my locker."

"Okay," Traci said, pausing with her hand on the door to the cafeteria, "I'll come with you."

43

"No, no," I said quickly. "You go ahead and save our table. I'll just be a second." I hurried away before she had a chance to protest.

I turned the corner and scanned the hall. Dave was standing at his open locker. I couldn't help noticing that his was a lot neater than Traci's was. "Dave," I said, tugging on his elbow.

"Oh, hey, Amanda," Dave said as he swung his locker shut. "What's up?" He raked his hair out of his eyes.

"I . . . well . . ." Now that I was here, I was unsure what to say. I cleared my throat and gave him a lop-sided smile. "It's kind of weird, isn't it?" I said finally.

"With Traci," Dave said, nodding. "Yeah."

I shrugged. "I just wanted to let you know—that I thought she was kind of harsh with you."

"Yeah, well." Dave smiled, and his brown eyes seemed to dance. "She is my sister, after all. That's pretty much how it's supposed to be."

I chuckled softly. "I guess I'm just not used to it," I said. My stepbrother and stepsister are four and total twin terrors. But since I'm so much older, I had been raised pretty much as an only child.

Dave leaned against his locker. "Maybe you'll *get* used to it," he said simply.

I felt a blush creep up the back of my neck. Did he mean that I should get used to it because I should get used to hanging with him? I really hoped so.

"But maybe we could do some stuff without Traci," Dave went on, jamming his fists into his pockets. He stared at his shoes, then glanced up at me shyly. "What are you doing after school today?"

"I don't have any plans," I said breathlessly. My heart thudded in my chest.

"Great!" Dave said with a grin. "Maybe we could grab some pizza or something?"

"Sure," I said quickly. "I love pizza!" Oh, ugh. I wanted to smack myself on the forehead over how dumb that sounded, but Dave just laughed.

"Me too," he said. "I'll come by your locker later."

"Okay," I told him. "See you then."

I couldn't stop smiling as I gave him a little wave and jogged off toward the cafeteria. Wow—that had certainly turned out better than I expected! I mean, this was sort of a date. Wasn't it? A kind of, almost date. Anyway, even if it was just pizza at Sal's, I knew that it would be fun, and it would be a chance to talk to Dave without worrying about Traci. After all, she'd be busy running errands with her mom all afternoon. This was just . . . perfect!

I smiled at Traci, who was still in the lunch line, as I hurried toward our usual table. Arielle was there already, sipping orange juice from a small carton.

"Hi," I said as I slid into the seat across from hers.

"What are you grinning about?" Arielle asked.

"Oh, nothing," I said as I pulled my sandwich

from my brown bag. I didn't feel like telling Arielle about Dave right then. I'd tell her later—when Traci wasn't about to come over with her tray. I couldn't stop smiling, though. I still had a grin on my face as I took a bite of my tuna sandwich.

The corners of Arielle's mouth tucked into a frown, and her eyes flashed dangerously. "So," she snapped, "don't you have anything to say to me?"

I had to force myself to chew—the tuna suddenly tasted like Styrofoam in my mouth. Arielle was clearly mad at me, but why? I pulled out a bottle of water and took a sip to force the tuna down. "What do you mean?" I asked.

"Don't you think you owe me an apology?" Arielle demanded. My face must have looked blank because she added, "For saying that soccer isn't important?"

"What?" I gasped. "Are you *serious?*"

"Do I look like I'm joking?" Arielle barked.

I rolled my eyes. "Forget it, Arielle," I said. I couldn't believe this! Arielle knew how important the arts were to me—did she seriously expect me to say that I thought sports deserved the funding more? "I think that *you* owe *me* an apology."

"In your dreams," Arielle shot back.

"You always have to get your way, don't you?" I asked.

Arielle slammed her drink carton down onto her tray. "What's *that* supposed to mean?" she almost shouted.

I was dimly aware that we were drawing stares from kids at nearby tables, but I didn't care. "It means that you're always thinking of yourself, whether it comes to uniforms or hogging the ball or whatever."

"Hogging the ball?" Arielle shrieked.

"That's right," I said. "You'd rather lose the game to Stanton than let someone else take the shot," I told her. "Just like you'd rather watch the arts funding get cut than wait another year for a new uniform!"

Arielle's face turned red, but I couldn't tell whether she was embarrassed or furious. Maybe a little of both. "I didn't let Traci take that shot because she was too distracted by her crush to make it!" she growled.

A tray slammed onto the table, and we both looked up into Traci's glowering face. My heart sank. Why had I brought up that stupid Stanton game? Now Traci was furious. "I would have made that shot," Traci insisted.

"Oh, *please*," Arielle said, flipping her hair over her shoulder. "You were too busy making googly eyes at Ryan to have your head in the game."

"I wasn't making googly eyes at anyone!" Traci cried. "So I missed a goal—so what? You missed one, too!"

Arielle shrugged. "Whatever," she said, pretending to study her fingernails.

I could see the muscles in Traci's jaw working like mad as she scooped up her tray and stormed off.

"What are you doing?" I whispered to Arielle. "You should apologize to her!"

"Is that your business?" Arielle demanded. She leaned forward and pointed at me. "Listen, Amanda. You should be on my side, not Traci's. You know that what I said was true. Besides, I am sick and tired of you picking your other friends over me. Are we best friends or aren't we?"

I stared at her finger, which was about an inch from my nose. It was taking all of my willpower not to slap it away. *Why does she always insist that she's right when she's so clearly wrong?* I wondered. *How can she treat her friends this way?* "I guess I really don't know anymore," I said quietly.

Arielle sat perfectly still for a moment, almost as if she hadn't understood what I'd said. Finally, it seemed to sink in, and her face clouded over. "Fine," she said quietly. She grabbed her tray and stood up. "I guess I'll see you around, Amanda."

"Hey, Arielle," Felicia said as she put down her tray. But Arielle just ignored her and stalked off.

Felicia turned to me, her dark eyes wide. "What did I do?" she asked.

I shrugged. "Nothing," I said. "It's about me, not you."

Felicia chewed a fingernail. "Is everything okay?" she asked. "What's going on?"

I sighed. It was a good question. What *was* going on? Had I really just ended my friendship with

Arielle? We'd had fights before, but I'd never had any doubts about her being my best friend. Still, I had to hope that Arielle would come to her senses and see that I was right. Although I didn't have much hope that would happen. Arielle could be stubborn when she felt like it. *Very* stubborn. "Felicia," I told her as I shook my head, "you don't want to know."

chapter
SIX

Amanda's diary entry

<u>WHAT I LIKE ABOUT DAVE:</u>
1. HE'S NICE TO ANIMALS EVEN THOUGH HE'S TOTALLY ALLERGIC TO THEM.
2. HIS HAIR FLOPS IN HIS EYES. CUTE!
3. HE HAS A GREAT SMILE.
4. HE DOESN'T ACT LIKE HE THINKS HE'S COOLER THAN ME JUST BECAUSE HE'S OLDER.
5. HE'S FUNNY.
6. HE DOESN'T START FOOD FIGHTS IN THE LUNCHROOM.

<u>WHAT I DON'T LIKE ABOUT DAVE:</u>
1. FEELING LIKE AN AWKWARD FREAKAZOID WHENEVER TRACI IS AROUND.

"Do you know what kind of pizza you're getting?" Dave asked as he scanned the menu.

I didn't even need to open mine. "Veggie," I said automatically. "And a diet Sprite." That was pretty much my standard order at Wonder Lake Pizza.

Dave grinned and leaned back against the red vinyl booth. "You don't even need to think about it?" he asked. "There's at least thirty different kinds of pizza on the menu."

"I know what I like," I told him, and he laughed.

"Hi—are you guys ready to order?" The waitress pulled a pencil from her disheveled-looking bun. She was only a few years older than we were and looked like she was having a pretty rough day. I could understand why—school had only been out for thirty minutes, but already the place was packed.

I gave the waitress my order, and she scribbled it onto a small pad.

"And . . . I'll have . . . hmmm . . ." Dave frowned at the menu. "How's the Hawaiian pizza?"

The waitress shrugged. "No idea. This is my first day, actually. But lots of people have been ordering it, so it must be good, right?"

"Okay," Dave said. "I'll have that, then. And a Coke."

The waitress nodded and walked away.

"Hawaiian pizza?" I said once the waitress was out of earshot. "You're brave. Isn't that ham and pineapple?"

"Yeah," Dave said. "I know. It sounds kind of gross, right?"

I crinkled my nose. "So why did you order it?"

"I don't know," Dave said, pushing his blond bangs

51

out of his eyes. "I mean—maybe it's good. And if it's bad, at least I'll have a funny story to tell my friends tomorrow."

I thought about that for a moment. "That makes sense," I told him, "in a weird kind of way." Suddenly, I wished I had ordered something different from my usual veggie pizza. Why did I always get the same thing, anyway?

"Here you go," the waitress said as she slid two paper plates in front of us and plunked our sodas on the table. "One triple cheese with olives and one slice of white pizza. Enjoy." She hurried away before we could say anything. I looked at the drinks. One was a root beer, and the other was an orange soda.

"Wow," Dave said. "It really *is* her first day, isn't it?"

I giggled. "I've never seen anyone get an order *this* wrong before. Um, should we call her over?" I twisted in my seat, looking for the waitress, but she had disappeared into the back.

Dave lifted his shoulders and let them drop. "Personally, I don't really care. I love orange soda."

"And I love root beer." I smiled and reached for the drink.

"Do you want to divide up these slices?" Dave asked. "Half of each?"

"Sounds good," I told him. "I've always been curious about the white pizza, anyway."

Dave cut both slices in half and let me choose

which ones I wanted. "Mmm," I said as I bit into the white pizza. It was made with ricotta and mozzarella cheese and didn't have any tomato sauce, so it tasted different from regular pizza. But it was still delicious.

"This is really good," Dave said as he bit into his olive slice. "I love olives. They should be, like, their own food group."

"I agree." I couldn't help smiling as I watched Dave take a sip of his orange soda. *If I had been here with Arielle*, I thought, *she would have freaked when the waitress mixed up our order.* But Dave made it seem— fun. Almost as though the waitress had brought us a special treat.

"So—" Dave said, wiping his mouth with a napkin, "you've been working on the spirit mural, right? I was thinking I'd go over and help out sometime next week."

I grimaced. "Actually, I think the project is on hold for a while."

"Really?" Dave frowned. "Why?"

I sighed and pushed my plate away. My appetite had suddenly disappeared. "The school board is planning to cut the arts budget. And there are practically no supplies whatsoever."

Dave stopped midchew and stared at me for a moment. "You're kidding," he said.

I shook my head. "I wish I were kidding. They want to give the money to the athletics department."

"I can't believe it," Dave said. His face had turned pale, and his freckles stood out dark against his skin. "The students can't just let this happen," he said, pounding the table decisively. "We have to do something—something huge—to get their attention."

"Like what?" I asked. I couldn't stop myself from grinning a little at his enthusiasm.

"Like a sit-in," Dave said. "Or we'll picket. We'll organize the entire student body!" His expression was so earnest that it actually made me laugh out loud. "What's so funny?" Dave asked. He looked a little hurt.

"I'm sorry," I said quickly. "Actually, those are great ideas. But I don't think we need to go that far. The school board is having a meeting next week, and I'm going to make a presentation about the arts." I fiddled with my straw wrapper. "If I do a decent job, they may decide not to cut the budget." I decided not to add that if I didn't do a decent job, the budget was toast.

"That's a great idea," Dave said. "Just let me know what I can do to help."

"Really?" I asked with a smile.

"Of course," Dave said. "Art is really important to me."

I looked at him for a moment, surprised by how serious his expression was. "I never knew you were so interested in art," I said, secretly wondering whether Dave was worried about his mother losing her job. Not that his reason for caring mattered to me. I was just glad that he wanted to help. Part of me couldn't

54

believe that Dave cared more about helping me than two of my BFFs did.

Dave raked a hand through his hair. I was beginning to recognize that as a nervous habit of his. "Amanda," he said slowly, "there's something I want to show you. It's at my house."

His face was hopeful. I knew that he wanted me to say that I would come over, but I hesitated. For some reason, the idea of going over to Traci's house and not hanging out with Traci seemed . . . strange. Then again, it was still early. She probably wasn't home yet. And Dave looked so eager. Really, how in the world could I say no?

"Okay," I said. "Let's go."

"Mom?" Dave called as he pushed open the front door. "Traci?" No response. "Come on in," Dave said to me.

I followed him into the quiet house. It was strange. Even though I had been here lots of times, I felt like I was seeing the McClintic house for the first time. I was surprised by a small painting of a sunset on the wall in the foyer. Even though I usually preferred art that was less realistic and more interpretive, I had to admit that the colors were beautiful. Why hadn't I ever noticed it before?

"I'll be right back," Dave said as he hurried up the stairs to his room.

I wandered into the living room and sat down at the black upright piano, letting my fingers wander idly over the ivory piano keys. I pressed one, and a rich note rang through the room. There were more landscapes on the walls in here, and the bookcases were lined with hardcover fiction. The arts were everywhere in the McClintic house. I guess that made sense, given that Ms. McClintic's career was music.

My eye fell on a picture of Traci in a silver frame, and I sighed. I wished that she were backing me up on the arts budget. It was definitely strange to feel that I had more support from Dave than I did from her.

Footsteps thundered down the stairs, and a moment later Dave rushed into the living room, staggering slightly under the weight of an enormous stack of papers.

"What is that?" I asked as he plopped them down on the coffee table.

Dave pulled a few booklets off the top and fanned them out. They were filled with rows and rows of colorful boxed illustrations. He smiled at me and gave a little "ta-da" gesture.

"Comic books?" I said, giving him a confused half smile, half frown.

"Yeah," Dave said eagerly. "I draw them."

"You do?" I asked, staring at the comics in surprise. I couldn't believe it—they looked so professional! I sat down on the couch to look at them more closely. "Wow," I whispered as I flipped through the one on top.

"You like them?" Dave asked, running a hand through his hair. I couldn't help noticing that he was blushing slightly and grinning from ear to ear.

"These are amazing!" I said, and I really meant it. "How long have you been doing this?"

"Oh—I don't know." Dave thought for a moment. "Maybe four years? Me and my good friend Blake used to make them back in Charleston. But now—it's just me. Ever since we moved to Wonder Lake, I'm a one-man comic machine."

I picked up another comic and stared at the cover. The superhero on the front seemed to be flying directly at me. I could feel Dave's eyes on me as I turned the pages, which were packed with illustration after illustration. I don't know much about comic books, but I know good art when I see it. There was no doubt about it—Dave was really talented. "This is great!" I told him. "I can't believe I never even knew you could draw!"

Dave jammed his hands in his pockets, clearly embarrassed. "Oh, well . . . ," he said. "You know, it's just something I do by myself. But still." He looked at me, his gaze even. "It's really important to me. It kept me sane when everything else was driving me crazy, you know?"

I nodded. I knew exactly what he meant.

"And that's why I want to help you make your presentation to the school board," Dave went on. "I'll help in any way I can, Amanda. You just name it."

"Really?" I breathed. "That would be great!" I had to resist the urge to give him a hug. I really wanted to, but I wasn't sure how he would react. "Maybe we could even use your comics."

Dave's eyebrows knit together in confusion. "How?"

"We could make a comic-book-style pamphlet," I said, the idea taking shape in my mind as I spoke. "About the benefits of an arts education. It would definitely be better than a boring old handout, which was what I was going to give them."

"That's a great idea!" Dave said.

Just then a key rattled in the door. "Dave?" called a voice. It was Ms. McClintic.

"In here," Dave called.

A moment later Ms. McClintic walked into the living room. She was carrying a bunch of hangers covered in plastic. Traci walked in a moment after her, holding a paper grocery bag. Traci saw me and smiled, then noticed Dave and frowned slightly. My stomach gave a nervous little lurch. I had been so excited about Dave's comics that my strange feelings about being in Traci's house had completely disappeared. But now they were back—big time.

Ms. McClintic smiled at me. "Hello, Amanda," she

said. "What are you doing here?"

"Amanda and I are working on a presentation for the school board," Dave said. "They want to cut the arts budget."

"Oh, I know." Ms. McClintic shook her head. "It's dreadful. I'm so glad the two of you are going to try to do something." She glanced at Traci, who turned beet red and looked at her shoes. Ms. McClintic waited a moment, as if she expected Traci to say that she was going to help, too, but Traci didn't say a word. "Well," Ms. McClintic said, lifting her eyebrows, "I guess I'd better go put this dry cleaning away. It was nice seeing you, Amanda." Ms. McClintic turned and headed up the stairs, leaving Dave and me alone with Traci. For a moment nobody spoke.

Awkwardness washed over me like a wave. Traci was still staring at the floor, and I felt like I needed to say something to ease the tension. I wanted to explain what I was doing here with Dave. I felt like I needed a good excuse for coming over for any reason other than to see Traci. "So—uh, you know, the school board is meeting really soon," I said quickly, "so Dave and I just decided that we needed to get to work—"

"Yeah, well, I guess I'll be too busy with soccer to help you guys." Traci's voice was harsh as she looked me in the eye.

I gulped. Oh, no! Did Traci think that I was trying to make her feel guilty for not helping us? That wasn't what I meant at all! I just wanted her to know why I was here. . . . I racked my brain for something to say that would fix the situation. Desperate, I looked at Dave, but he was studying his shoes as if he thought they might have the secret to life printed on them.

Traci looked around, and her eye fell on Dave's comic books. "Ugh, what are these lame things doing out?" she asked, rolling her eyes.

Dave didn't say anything, but I noticed a red blush beginning to creep up his neck. He ran a hand through his hair and kept his eyes on his sneakers.

"Actually, I was looking at them," I said to Traci. "I think they're really good."

Traci gaped at me a moment, and I had to force myself not to cringe under her gaze. "Yeah, well . . ." she said after an awkward pause, "I guess I'd better put these groceries away. I'll see you, Amanda."

"See you," I called softly after Traci as she walked out of the room. I looked at Dave, and he gave me a lopsided smile. I tried to smile back, but I think it came out more like a grimace. The way Traci had looked at me—it was almost as if she thought I was a traitor. It was exactly the way that Arielle had looked at me at lunch. And it was really beginning to worry me.

chapter
SEVEN

Amanda:

I humbly accept this opportunity to be part of your state-of-the-arts presentation. I only hope that my meager skills will in some way help to enlighten the ever-foggy school board as to the value of the arts. It is an important issue. Speaking of important issues, do you think that we can get the cafeteria to stop serving the special sauce ON the fish sticks for lunch? It's really annoying to try to scrape it off—it always leaves a faint green snotlike glob.

Respectfully yours,

Ryan

I stamped my feet and pulled my orange-and-pink-striped scarf tight around my neck. Penny had given me the scarf for Christmas last year, and I absolutely loved it. It was the softest scarf I had ever owned, and it was hand-knit by a friend of Penny's. I was glad that I had remembered to wear it this morning—the weather had dropped suddenly overnight, and now we were into the real December temperatures.

"Are you sure Penny knows to pick us up here?"

Felicia asked. Her dark eyes peeked out from her hood, which was lined with fake fur. Small puffs of steam streamed from her mouth at every breath.

"Definitely," I said. "She's running a little late, that's all."

Felicia harrumphed, and I checked my watch for about the zillionth time. The truth was, Penny was more than a little late. She was almost twenty minutes late, which was pretty unusual for her. But sometimes she got really into her art and forgot to look at a clock or whatever. I mean, I couldn't really blame her for that. Then again, maybe we should have waited for her in the front hall of the school instead of on the steps. I was just about to suggest that we go inside when Penny's car drove up. I saw her tap the horn once and wave.

"Ugh, we can see you," Felicia muttered as we headed down the stairs. "You don't have to honk at us."

Oblivious to Felicia's gripes, Penny rolled down her window. "Hey!" she called, giving us a big smile. "Sorry I'm late, you guys! I hope you weren't waiting too long."

"Not too long," I said as I opened the passenger side door.

"Almost half an hour," Felicia said as she slid into the seat behind Penny.

Penny grimaced at Felicia in the rearview mirror. "Half an hour? Really? Gosh, I'm so sorry about that!"

Felicia shrugged and looked out the window. "No big deal," she said, although her tone of voice implied that it *was* a big deal. She rubbed her mittened hands together and blew on them.

"It wasn't quite half an hour," I put in quickly. I didn't want Penny to feel like she had abandoned us in Siberia or something. "More like twenty minutes. But it kind of felt like half an hour in that cold!" I looked at Felicia, but she just rolled her eyes. I sighed. I mean, I knew that she wasn't crazy about Penny, but everyone is late sometimes. Still, I had to be careful. I didn't want to start an argument with Felicia. After all, she was coming over to help me with the arts budget presentation, and I was really, really grateful.

"You must be freezing. Here, let me turn up the heat," Penny said, turning one of the dials on the dashboard. "This should unfreeze you a little." Penny pulled the car away from the curb. "So—what are you guys up to this afternoon? Fun plans?"

I rubbed a patch of fog from my window so that I could watch the trees pass by. "Not exactly." I explained about the arts budget and how we had to plan a presentation to stop it from getting cut. "Nandi and Dave are meeting us at my house," I said, "so we can brainstorm a few ideas."

Penny shook her head. "I can't believe they're going to cut the budget—just like that! I'm so glad you two are going to try to stop them." She smiled at Felicia in the rearview mirror.

Felicia bit her lip. "I just hope it works," she said thoughtfully. "My dad always says that you can't fight city hall."

"That's what city hall *wants* you to think," Penny countered. Felicia smiled wryly and looked out the window. "Anyway, I don't think you'll be sorry that you tried," Penny went on, "even if they do end up making the cuts. So—what are your plans for the presentation?"

"We aren't really sure yet," I told her, hesitating. I hadn't run the comic book pamphlet by Felicia yet, and I wasn't sure what she would think of the idea. But I decided to toss it out there. After all, it would be better to know what she thought of the idea now, before we were in a room with Dave. "You know Traci's brother, Dave? Well, he makes these way cool comic books. Anyway, I was thinking that we could make a comic-style pamphlet to go with our presentation."

"That sounds like a great idea," Penny said, smiling enthusiastically.

"Yeah," Felicia agreed quickly, then frowned. "But wait—doesn't color printing cost a ton of money?" I knew what she was thinking: Who would pay?

"You're right," I said, bummed. "I hadn't even thought of that, but I think it can run up to a dollar a page."

Penny waved her hand dismissively. "Don't worry about that," she said. "My cousin Dan runs a copy shop. I can get you the copies for free."

"Really?" I asked.

"Cool." Felicia smiled at Penny in the rearview mirror, and she smiled back.

"Hey, it looks like the troops are already here," Penny said as we pulled into my family's circular driveway. Dave and Nandi were standing on the front steps. When Dave saw us, he gave us a huge smile and waved. I waved back, grinning like crazy.

I couldn't wait to get started on our presentation. For the first time, I felt like we really had a chance to get the funding. A good chance. All it would take was a little work.

An hour and a half later I wasn't feeling so hopeful anymore. "Ugh, we've gone over this a thousand times," I said, shoving my yellow legal pad across the coffee table. I had been taking notes, but so far, there wasn't much on the pad except for a doodle of a palm tree. "And we're still nowhere."

"I still say that a presentation about the arts should be interesting," Dave said. He leaned back in my dad's favorite overstuffed armchair. "It shouldn't just be a bunch of facts and graphs and stuff like that."

"But we *need* the facts," Nandi argued from her spot on the couch. We had all taken off our shoes and socks, and Nandi's bare feet were tucked delicately beneath her. "The school board isn't going to just give us money for being creative."

"There has to be a way to do both." Felicia rested her chin in her hands. She was lying on the floor. Her forehead was creased with concentration, and I could tell that she was thinking hard.

"This is totally making my brain hurt," I said, putting my hands to the sides of my head. "I feel like my head is about to explode."

"No exploding heads," Penny joked from the doorway. "It makes too much of a mess." She was holding a wooden tray, on top of which were four steaming mugs and a plate of sugar cookies. "How's it going?" she asked as she slid the tray onto the coffee table and everyone gathered around.

"Much better, now that there's cookies involved," Dave said, reaching for one.

"Mmm, cocoa," Nandi said. She took a quick sip and licked the chocolate mustache off her upper lip.

"Made any progress?" Penny asked, eyeing the palm tree on my legal pad.

"Not much," I admitted. "We know what we want to say—we just can't figure out how to say it."

Penny laughed.

"What's so funny?" Felicia asked.

"Oh—nothing," Penny said, lifting her shoulders in a slight shrug. "It's just . . . that's kind of the whole

66

problem of art, isn't it? I mean, often artists are trying to express similar things. But it's the differences in how it's done that make art interesting."

Felicia looked thoughtful as she took a bite of her sugar cookie.

"Okay," I said, taking a sip of my cocoa, "so what should we do?"

"Have you tried giving up?" Penny asked.

I stared at her in disbelief. "Give up?"

"No way!" Dave cried.

Penny's eyes were dancing. "I don't mean permanently," she explained. "I just mean for a few minutes. Sometimes when I'm stuck and my work isn't going anywhere, I just leave it and do something completely different. Then when I focus on the problem again, I can usually come up with a new solution."

"So—what should we do?" Felicia asked. The corners of her mouth were tucked into a doubtful frown.

Penny walked over to the stereo and punched the power button. Then she turned up the volume until loud hip-hop music was pouring from the speakers. "Let's dance!" she yelled over the music. Penny bobbed up and down and shook her head from side to side. Her long hair flared wildly. "Come on!"

Nandi giggled and got up from the couch. She did a graceful pirouette and then a few small leaps. All of those ballet classes had paid off—Nandi was a terrific dancer.

"Up here!" Dave cried. He took my hand and pulled me up onto the couch. We started jumping up and down as Penny and Nandi twirled around the room. Felicia stared at them, wide-eyed, as the loud music throbbed through the room.

"Come on, Felicia!" I urged. "It's fun!"

Felicia shook her head. "No—I—"

But Nandi grabbed Felicia's hands and swept her into a tango. Felicia and Nandi strutted across the living room. "Olé!" Nandi cried as they turned back and strutted the other way.

Felicia giggled as the music changed to a quicker beat. Soon she was bobbing around the room, her long dark hair spreading around her like a fan.

I whooped and punched my fist in the air, then leaped over the back of the couch. Dave followed, and soon we were running madly around the room. I laughed out loud. This was so much fun!

"Wait a minute!" Felicia cried suddenly. "Everyone stop!" She waved her hands frantically, and Penny turned off the stereo.

"What's up?" I asked, shoving a few sweaty strands of hair off my forehead.

"Music!" Felicia cried. She was grinning from ear to ear, as if she had just discovered electricity or the wheel or something.

"Um—yeah?" Dave asked. "You just made us turn it off, remember?"

"No, no." Felicia shook her head impatiently. "Not that music. I mean, the *presentation* should have music." Her cheeks flushed pink as her words poured out in a rush. "I could play my flute, and maybe we could get Ryan to play the violin . . ."

"Great idea!" I cried. Ryan was an excellent violinist.

". . . and not only that, we could have other kinds of art, too!" Felicia went on eagerly. "Amanda would start her presentation, and Ryan and I could play something, and Nandi, maybe you would dance, and Dave, you could put up a large painting behind Amanda. And then Amanda—when you're finished, you could say, 'Imagine a world without art,' and Ryan and I could stop playing, and Nandi would stop dancing, and Dave would throw a cloth over the painting—"

"Ohmigosh, I have to write this down!" I cried, diving for the yellow pad.

Suddenly, everyone started talking at once. Nandi knew exactly what piece she would perform, and Dave said that he thought we could use one of his family's paintings. I had to write like crazy to get all of the ideas down, they were flowing so quickly. But I didn't mind. We were finally on track!

As I was writing, I looked up at Felicia. I wanted to tell her thank you, but she wasn't really paying attention to me. Instead she was grinning at Penny, who was positively grinning back. And who could blame them? After all, Penny's idea had succeeded—we'd taken a break, had fun, and come up with a great idea! And I knew the presentation would work now. I just knew it.

After all—it had to.

chapter
EIGHT

E-mails sent and received Friday night:

To: PrincessA
From: FiFiol
  Hi! Call me L8R—can't wait to tell u about the presentation. Penny came up with some great ideas!

To: FiFiol
From: PrincessA
  You mean to tell me Penny finally let some air out of her head to leave room for a good idea? :o)

To: PrincessA
From: FiFiol
  Yeah, actually, she was pretty cool tonight.
  I mean, she's still kind of a flake. LOL. But when it comes to the arts, maybe being a flake is okay sometimes?

To: FiFiol
From: PrincessA
  I'll have to talk 2 u tomorrow. Got a ton
of reading 2 do for English.

To: PrincessA
From: FiFiol
  Oh. Okay. C u tomorrow, then. . . .

"Hey, Arielle, need some help?" I asked. We were at
Mr. Fiol's animal shelter, and Arielle was struggling
to get Buster, the seriously squirmy black puppy who
had dunked himself in mud earlier in the week, into
the dog carrier. It was Saturday, and we were about
to head over to the Wonder Lake Hospital for
Healing Paws.

"I've got it," Arielle snapped as Buster twisted in
her hands. She was trying to open the dog carrier
with her elbow. It wasn't working.

"Let me get that," I said, flipping open the latch.

Arielle grunted—in thanks, I guess—and set
Buster gently into the carrier. She didn't even glance
at me. I breathed deeply, trying not to let my frustra-
tion show. After all, I was *trying* to be nice. After my
arts budget brainstorming session the day before, I'd
felt so good that I'd decided I needed to make up
with Arielle. After all, she was entitled to her opinion,
wasn't she? I knew that sports were as important to

her as the arts were to me—so I could respect her stance. But she had barely said a word to me all day. I decided to try again. "So," I began, "I didn't see you at lunch yesterday."

"I've been busy," Arielle said with a shrug. She flipped her long, smooth hair over her shoulder and folded her arms across her chest.

Grrr. Why was she making this so hard? Arielle is my oldest friend—and she knows exactly how to make me crazy. *Fine,* I thought, folding my arms across my chest and imitating Arielle's stance, *if she doesn't want to talk to me, then I won't talk to her, either.*

"Okay, guys, ready to go?" Felicia asked as she walked out of the shed with a cat carrier, which held two fluffy guinea pigs. Traci was behind her, holding a rabbit in her arms. Felicia looked from Arielle's face to mine and frowned. I knew that she could tell we were fighting. I guess it was pretty obvious.

"Amanda, would you help me with Lester?" Traci asked, looking down at the rabbit.

"Sure," I replied. I took Lester from Traci. The rabbit kicked a little before settling down, then let me stroke his silky ears while Traci opened his carryall. I let Lester hop inside, then flipped the latch closed behind him.

"Ready to go, girls?" Mr. Fiol asked as he walked up to the van, jingling his car keys. He opened the doors at the back.

"Where's Penny?" Traci asked as she carefully placed Lester's carryall in the van. "Isn't she coming?"

"Penny can't make it today," I explained. "One of her art students had to reschedule a lesson, and the only time he could see her was this morning. She'll be back next week, though."

Mr. Fiol was whistling as he got behind the steering wheel. I smiled at Felicia, who smiled back. Mr. Fiol could be kind of stern and strict, but he had loosened up a little ever since he had met Penny. "So, I hear you girls are taking on the school board," Mr. Fiol said to me as he backed out of the driveway and pulled onto the street. "Penny tells me that you've come up with some great ideas."

"Yeah, Penny really helped us," Felicia admitted. "And we had a lot of fun."

Wow, I thought. Was this really Felicia? She'd never had anything nice to say about Penny before. Maybe this whole arts budget presentation would have some positive effects beyond the ones I'd been hoping for.

I glanced at Arielle, who was staring out the window, scowling. But Traci looked kind of interested.

"What's the big plan?" Traci asked.

"Well, we're going to get some of the kids who are good in the arts to help us. Nandi is going to dance, and Felicia is going to play the flute. And I got an e-mail from Ryan last night—he's going to play the violin."

"Really?" Traci said faintly, but the corners of her mouth had flickered down.

"Uh—yeah," I said, suddenly uncomfortable. Gosh—had I said the wrong thing? I'd thought that Traci would be interested to hear about Ryan.

Felicia looked back at me uneasily from her place in the front seat. I pressed my lips together. Now both Traci and Arielle were staring out the window. I guessed that we should stop talking about the arts presentation. It didn't seem like Traci or Arielle wanted to hear about it. Silence filled the van like air in a balloon.

I couldn't help wondering how much pressure we could take before we popped.

"Okay," Felicia said, scanning her list of kids who had signed up for Healing Paws. "The guinea pigs should go to see Matt Field and Sally Mickle. Buster is here for Samantha Petra. And Lester goes to Annmarie Salis."

"Got it," I said, glancing at Arielle. I figured that she would want to take Buster to Samantha. Sam was one of Arielle's favorite patients. She was eight years old, and she had non-Hodgkin's lymphoma, which is a kind of cancer, so she was in and out of the hospital a lot. Her treatments were tough on her, but she always had a smile on her face. And she was crazy about Buster. Last week Sam had begged Arielle to let her sign up first on the Healing Paws sheet so that she could request him.

"Traci and I will take the guinea pigs," Felicia went on. "Why don't you two take Buster and then come back for Lester?" Felicia smiled hesitantly at me.

I shook my head slightly. I knew what she was trying to do. Felicia knew that Arielle and I had been fighting—so she figured that if the two of us spent some time together, we'd make up. That just goes to show that Felicia doesn't know Arielle nearly as well as I do. My oldest friend has a stubborn streak a mile wide.

"Sounds good," Traci said, heaving the carryall with the guinea pigs inside.

"Fine," Arielle snapped. She grabbed the handle of Buster's carrying case, and he let out a small bark.

We didn't say a word as we walked down the long white hallway toward Sam's room. I knocked gently on her door, which was covered in pictures that Sam had drawn.

"Come in!" Samantha sang, and I pushed open the door. "Is it Buster?" she asked eagerly when she saw the carryall in Arielle's hand.

Arielle couldn't help smiling. "It sure is," she said. "And I know he's going to be happy to see you."

"Buster!" Sam cried as I undid the latch and the puppy loped clumsily into her lap. "I missed you, too!" Buster was licking her face, and his tiny tail was wagging like crazy. "Hey, do you notice anything different about me?" Sam asked us as she stroked Buster's fur.

"Hmmm," Arielle said. "Well, your hair is starting to grow in." When we had visited the hospital the week before, Sam was completely bald from her chemotherapy treatments.

"Yeah!" Sam said with a laugh. "Blond! It used to be brown. My doctor told me he knew someone who had red hair that turned black."

"Wow," I said. "Well, they say that blonds have more fun."

Sam giggled. "I hope it's true!"

I smiled at her. I couldn't believe that she was so upbeat. She played with Buster for about half an hour. Finally a nurse with red hair named Diandra poked her head in.

"Hi, Amanda. Hi, Arielle," she said. "I'm sorry, but the doctor will be here in a few minutes to see Sam. The puppy should probably go now."

Sam let out a disappointed groan, but Arielle patted her leg and said, "No, that's okay. We have to take a bunny to see another little girl right now, anyway. You can spend more time with Buster another day."

"Can I sign up to see Buster again next week?" Sam asked, looking up at Arielle with big brown eyes.

Arielle grinned at her. "Don't tell anyone," she said, "but I already put you on the list."

"You did? Oh, thanks, Arielle!" Sam said. "You guys are the best!"

We said good-bye and followed the nurse into the hall. "Sam just loves that puppy," Diandra said as she closed Sam's door. She pointed to a picture Sam had drawn of a smiling black puppy. *Buster* was written beneath it.

"She's done a lot of drawings," Arielle remarked, staring at the door. It was true. It was covered in all kinds of pictures—of her family, of a stick-figure Sam standing beside a house, and at least three more of Buster.

"Yes—Sam's treatments make her weak," Diandra explained. "It's hard for her to play with other children, but she loves to draw. And it's a way for her to remember the things that make her happy."

Arielle traced her fingers over the drawing of Buster, frowning thoughtfully. She turned and caught me watching her. But she didn't snap at me this time. Instead she said, "I'm glad we came here," in a quiet voice.

I nodded.

Arielle didn't say anything else and neither did I as we walked together down the hallway. I thought about how sweet Arielle had been with Sam. That's the thing about Arielle—she can be stubborn, but she can be kind, too. And usually the kindness outweighs the stubbornness. *Usually.*

I sneaked a sideways glance at her as we walked side by side, but I couldn't read her expression. *Does she miss me as much as I miss her?* I wondered. But I didn't dare ask. There was really only one way to deal with Arielle's anger, and that was to wait it out. So that was what I'd have to do.

I just hoped that I wouldn't be waiting forever.

chapter
NINE

E-mail received Monday morning:

From: Sk8boy
To: FlowerGrl

Amanda,

Just wanted to warn you—tonight at dinner there were some serious fireworks between Traci and Mom. Mom announced that we were all going to the school board meeting to show our support for the arts budget, but Traci said she didn't want to go. Mom glared at her and said that she wasn't <u>asking</u>. (Whew!) Then Traci started stabbing at her salad like some crazed lettuce murderer. N e way, just thought you should know since T. may be in a baaaaaad mood the next time you see her. . . .

On the plus side, Penny came over and picked up the pamphlet. She says it should be printed by tomorrow. Let's hope this works!

Dave

Ohmigosh, I thought as I reread the e-mail, *Traci must be so mad at me!* It was my study hall period, and I was using one of the computers in the media lab to check my e-mail. Technically, we weren't supposed to use school computers for anything but schoolwork, but this time I was happy that I had. *No wonder Traci was so quiet during lunch*, I realized. *She probably thinks that her fight with her mom is all my fault. And it kind of is. After all, if Dave and I weren't working on the arts budget presentation, Ms. McClintic wouldn't be angry that Traci wasn't helping.*

Guilt fluttered in my stomach, and I glanced up at the clock, willing the hands to move faster. I had to talk to Traci—I wanted to apologize right away! The fact was, I really understood why Traci felt that she owed her allegiance to sports instead of arts. I knew that soccer was her thing and orchestra wasn't. But I *also* knew that it had to be hard for Ms. McClintic to understand that. *I never should have brought up the subject in front of the two of them*, I thought. *I should have just kept my mouth shut!* It was last period—maybe I could catch Traci at her locker before she went to soccer practice. After three excruciating minutes the bell *finally* rang, and I scooped up my books and hurried into the hall.

"Traci!" I called as soon as I saw her familiar blond ponytail. She was standing at her locker, fighting with a binder as usual.

"Amanda—hey," Traci said as I scurried up beside her. She frowned slightly. "Are you all right?"

"What? Oh, I'm fine," I said, tucking a long strand of hair behind my ear. I rubbed my clammy palm against the front of the Indian print skirt I was wearing. "Um—but how are *you?*"

"Me?" Traci asked, her eyebrows lifting in surprise. "I'm fine, I guess." She turned and gave her binder a yank. It came free suddenly, and some of the papers inside fell to the floor. We both bent to pick them up.

"Listen, I, uh, heard about the fight you had with your mom last night," I said as I gathered papers. "I just wanted you to know how sorry I am about that. I mean, uh, is there anything I can do to help?" Ugh. This was coming out so awkward. It was as if I couldn't make my mouth form the coherent thoughts that were in my brain.

Traci was staring at me, her eyebrows drawn together in confusion, so I barreled ahead. "You know, um, you can still join the presentation if you want to. I mean, if you think it would make your mom—"

"Wait a minute," Traci said, holding up her hand traffic cop style. "Back up. How do you know about the fight I had with my mom?"

"Well, Dave sent me this e-mail, and . . ." My voice trailed off.

Traci's eyes darkened and her nostrils flared. She

looked furious. "Wait—you're saying that Dave sent you an e-mail about me?"

"Well—kind of," I admitted. "He just wanted me to know that you might be in a bad mood. . . ."

"Kind of?" Traci's voice was shrill with anger. "Are you telling me that you two have been talking about me behind my back?"

I had to admit, when she put it that way, it sounded pretty bad. I could feel my cheeks flaming. "I—I—it wasn't really like that," I stammered.

"No?" Traci asked. She whipped the papers out of my hand and stood up. "How was it?"

Shakily, I got to my feet. "I—I—it was just—" I stammered. "He wanted me to know that you might be mad—"

"Let me tell you something, Amanda," Traci said as she stuffed the papers back into her binder. "I wasn't mad before, but I sure am now." She slammed her locker and stalked off down the hall.

I stared after her helplessly. What had I done? Of course, Traci had a point. If I knew that she'd been talking about me behind my back, I would have been mad, too. But on the other hand, I knew that Dave had only been trying to help. I massaged my temples. All of this friend drama was giving me a major headache.

"One of those days?" Felicia's voice joked behind me.

I turned and saw her standing with Patrick Flanigan. He was a grade above us, and he and Felicia had been hanging out together a lot lately. I gave them the best smile I could muster, which was, under the circumstances, hardly a smile at all. "Try one of those weeks. One of those *lifetimes.*"

"Oh, come on," Patrick said. "It can't be that bad."

I knew he was just trying to be encouraging, but I wasn't in the mood to be cheered up. "Believe me," I told him, "it can."

"What's going on?" Felicia asked, twirling her hair around her finger nervously.

I groaned and leaned against the bank of lockers. "It's just more of this arts budget nightmare," I explained. "If I had realized that this stuff might cost me all of my best friends, believe me—I would have stayed out of it."

"Did Arielle say something to you?" Felicia guessed.

"No." I shook my head. "This time it was Traci."

Felicia grimaced. "Yikes," she said.

"Tell me about it," I agreed. Fighting with my friends was awful—and it always left me feeling really tired. Now I felt like I was going to slide down the lockers and into a puddle all over the floor of the hall.

"That's rough," Patrick said. "It's really too bad when friends let stuff like this come between them." He turned to Felicia and smiled. "And just for the record, I hope that you guys get the funding."

Felicia grinned up at him.

"Listen, I've got to get going," Patrick said. "Basketball practice starts in five minutes. But good luck, okay?" He gave me an awkward little pat on the shoulder before turning and walking down the hallway.

Felicia was still smiling when he disappeared around the corner.

Her dreamy look made me laugh a little. "Look at you, smiley face," I teased.

Felicia giggled and slapped her palms to her face, which had turned bright pink. "I just can't help it!" she said.

"Hmmm," I said, waggling my eyebrows, "it sounds like someone is in *luuuv*."

Felicia laughed, and I felt the tension drain out of my body a little. It felt good to be talking about something other than the arts budget—for once.

"Well, I don't know about love," Felicia said, "but I think I've got a case of extreme like."

"Yeah?" I asked, pushing myself away from the lockers. Felicia and I fell into step down the hall.

Felicia nodded shyly. "Patrick is really sweet—and sensitive. I mean, he's on the basketball team, you know? Sports are important to him. But he cares about the arts, too."

"That's great," I said warmly. I meant it. Patrick seemed really nice, and I was glad that Felicia was getting to know him. It was obvious that they liked each other a lot.

The minute we walked through the front doors to the school, I heard the chirping beep of Penny's car horn. She waved at me and I waved back. "There's my ride," I said to Felicia.

"Tell Penny I said hi," Felicia said. She gave Penny a wave, and Penny tapped the horn again.

"Okay," I said, smiling. It was good that Felicia and Penny were getting along. At least one thing was going well lately.

I said good-bye to Felicia and yanked open the door to Penny's car. "Hey," I said as I slid into the passenger seat. "You sure look happy." Penny's face was flushed, and she was wearing a brilliant grin.

"Guess what I've got," Penny said.

"Um, the flu?" I joked.

Penny rolled her eyes and reached into the backseat. "Would I be smiling if I had the flu?" She pulled a sheet of paper off a stack and held it out to me. "Ta-da!"

I looked down at the full-color page, and my heart started racing. "Ohmigosh!" I cried. "It's Dave's comic!"

"Hot off the presses," Penny said, craning her neck so that she could look at it, too. "I just picked it up—I think it looks pretty good."

"It looks amazing," I said breathlessly. It really did. Dave had done a fantastic job on the comic, and it had reproduced well. The colors were vibrant and sharp. "This will definitely get the school board's attention."

"Let's hope," Penny agreed, holding up crossed fingers.

"Thank you so much," I whispered, leaning over to give her a hug.

"Oh, it's nothing," Penny said. She looked kind of embarrassed but happy. "I mean, I have an interest in the arts, you know? I need people to buy my work and sponsor my shows."

"Yeah, right," I said, smiling. "You're just doing this for yourself."

Penny laughed as she pulled away from the curb. "Yes, I am," she agreed. "I'm just selfish, that's all."

I grinned at her. Penny was one of the *least* selfish people I knew. And I was lucky to have her. *Maybe that's what I need to do*, I thought as we drove toward home, *focus on the people who are supporting me instead of the ones who are angry with me. After all, Felicia, Penny, Dave, and Nandi are helping with the presentation*. And I could sort out the stuff with Arielle and Traci later.

I just had to do one thing at a time.

chapter
TEN

Excerpt from Dave's comic, to be handed out at the school board meeting:

Oh, no! Commander Bland is trapped in Dr. Crock's tarantula-infested pit of doom! How will the commander escape? He has absolutely no idea! Not a clue. Nope—nothing is coming to him. Why not? Because Commander Bland never had arts education in school—and now he can't think creatively! That's right, research shows that arts education helps with originality and creative problem-solving skills. Too bad for Commander Bland . . . but lucky for the tarantulas, who are about to have a nice Bland meal!

". . . music helps with cognitive skills and has been shown to help increase test scores in math." I paused for a moment so that the audience could appreciate the beauty of the flute and violin duet that Ryan and Felicia were playing before continuing. "And dance is more than a form of artistic expression. It's also a form of physical education, strengthening the muscles along with the mind." Nandi leaped forward and pirouetted around me in a series of intricate twists and turns. Her feet moved so fast that my eyes could hardly keep up with them. "Imagine a world without art," I concluded, and silence seemed to ring through the room as Ryan and Felicia stopped playing and Nandi held her final pose.

The audience let out a whoop as they jumped to their feet, clapping wildly. We'd been perfect—we'd totally nailed the presentation! I could hardly control my grin as the audience continued to applaud.

Of course, the audience was only Penny and Dave—but it was still a start. We were in my family's living room, rehearsing the presentation. My dad and Adele were out at a dinner party, and they had taken Jessy and Joey with them, so we had the whole house to ourselves.

Now Dave stuck his fingers in his mouth and let out a loud whistle. "Encore!" he cried.

"No, no!" Ryan cried, playing a catchy little tune on his violin. "No more encores!"

"I agree," Felicia said, flopping on the couch. "We've done it six times—I think we've got it."

"Well . . ." I hesitated, glancing at my notes. Part of me wanted to go over the presentation just one more time. But a quick glance around the room told me that everyone else was tired.

"You guys look like you're ready for some pizza," Penny said.

"I'm always ready for pizza," Ryan said.

"Me too," Nandi agreed.

"I'll call Sal's," Penny said as she started toward the kitchen. "How many should we get? Two?"

"Two *larges*," Dave suggested. "All of this rehearsing has made me hungry."

I laughed. "You haven't done anything but sit on the couch!" I teased. Dave's only part in the presentation was to throw a black cloth over a painting at the end. He'd pantomimed it with us a couple of times, but then he said he felt kind of silly, so he volunteered to watch and make suggestions.

"Hey—couch sitting can really make you work up an appetite," Dave insisted.

"Okay, I'll get two larges," Penny said. "Be right back."

I put my notes back into their folder and joined Felicia and Dave on the couch while Ryan played something for us on his violin. It took me a minute to realize that it wasn't classical music at all—it was a song from the latest album by Tekka, one of my favorite pop groups.

"Where did you learn to play that?" I asked him.

Ryan gave me a lopsided grin and shrugged. "I didn't," he said. "Sometimes I can just hear something, and I'm able to play it." He played another little piece—the theme song to my favorite TV show. I laughed again. I was so glad that he was helping with the presentation. Ryan's goofiness made the whole thing feel a lot less frightening.

"That's amazing!" Nandi said.

"I live to amaze," Ryan replied with a sweeping bow.

Suddenly, the lights dimmed for a moment, then came back on again.

"Uh-oh," Ryan said. He crossed to the window and pushed back the curtain with his bow. "It looks like this thunderstorm is getting pretty serious." Fat raindrops splattered against the windowpane, and the wind howled as it tore through the trees.

"It's supposed to rain until midnight," Felicia said, and at that very moment the lights went out completely.

My pulse quickened—I couldn't see a thing. Even though I like to think of myself as a pretty brave person, I have to admit that I've never been a hundred percent comfortable in the dark. I blinked a few times, waiting for my eyes to adjust to the sudden darkness. Low thunder rolled outside, and the rain seemed to strike the window furiously.

A door creaked. For a moment my heart fluttered wildly, then I heard Penny's voice ask, "Is everyone okay?"

"Um—I think so. Did the lights go out, or have I suddenly gone blind?" Ryan asked.

"I think there are some flashlights in the cabinet," I said.

I could hear Penny feeling her way toward the

large TV cabinet. Then there were clunks of things being knocked over as she groped for the flashlights. "Ooh, sorry," Penny said after a particularly loud thunk.

"Did she just apologize to the stuff in the cabinet?" Felicia whispered to me, giggling.

I had to laugh. "Hey, can she help it if she's nice to inanimate objects?"

"Gotcha!" Penny cried. A moment later a beam of light cut across the room, giving off enough illumination to see by. I smiled at Dave, who was holding on to the arm of the couch with an iron grip. It looked like he hadn't been too crazy about the sudden darkness, either.

Penny handed the flashlight to Ryan, then clicked on another one. "I'm going to check the fuse box," Penny announced.

"Great idea," Ryan said. "And if you don't come back, we'll each come after you one by one until the psycho hiding in the basement finally reveals himself." Ryan stuck the flashlight beneath his chin and let out an evil laugh.

"Oh, Ryan," Penny said, tousling his hair. "You're so creative. I'll be back in a sec."

"Wow," Felicia said. I knew what she was thinking. There was no way I would have gone down into the basement alone after what Ryan had said. Penny was braver than I'd realized.

"Great, now let's tell ghost stories," Ryan said the minute Penny had left the room. He held the flashlight beneath his chin again. "I've got a good one." His distorted grin looked seriously creepy in the light. I gave a shudder. Personally, I wasn't wild about ghost stories, but I didn't want to look silly in front of everyone else. And I guess I wasn't the only one. Felicia scooted a little closer to me as Ryan started his tale.

"Once upon a time, there was a young man who went hiking in the forest—*alone*," Ryan said.

"Always a mistake," Nandi put in.

"Yeah," Dave agreed. "Especially when you're the main character in a ghost story."

"Do you mind?" Ryan asked. "Okay, so there was a young man, and he was in the forest, and as the sun began to set, he realized that he had no idea where he was. He stumbled on in the direction he thought he had come from, but it just led him deeper and deeper into the woods. By now it was completely dark. He couldn't even see his hand in front of his face." Ryan paused and looked around the room. Nandi was sitting at Felicia's feet, and she shifted her weight slightly so that she was partially leaning against Felicia's leg. Dave slid his hand into mine. I tried hard not to worry that my palm might be sweaty and gross or something.

"Suddenly, the guy saw a light a long way off," Ryan went on. "He started walking toward it, and soon he saw that the light came from a campfire. There was a strange old man with wild gray hair sitting by the fire, and when he smiled, he showed long, sharp teeth. 'Hello,' the old man said. 'Would you like to see what I can do with my razor-sharp claw?' The old man held up his hand. All five fingernails were inches long, curved, and razor sharp. 'Uh, no,' the young man said. 'Oh, but I insist,' the old man said, drawing closer. 'No thanks,' the young man said again, but the old man just grinned and raised his claw." Ryan paused again, lifting his hand dramatically. Just then thunder sounded outside and a flash of lightning lit up the windows. I tightened my grip on Dave's hand. Suddenly, I didn't care if he knew I was afraid. "'You will be amazed at what my claw can do,' the old man said. 'Now watch carefully . . .'" I flinched, afraid of what might come next. Giving us a crazy look, Ryan turned his head sideways. He reached toward his face with his clawlike hand and then . . . pretended to pick his nose!

"Ryan, that is disgusting!" Nandi cried.

"Boo!" Felicia yanked the throw pillow from behind her and tossed it at Ryan's head. He ducked, laughing.

"You think that's funny, but it's snot," Dave said.

Everyone groaned. "I haven't heard that joke since the second grade," I told him. Dave just smiled at me. He was still holding my hand.

"Okay, everyone—I have some good news and

some bad news," Penny said as she walked into the room. She sat down on the arm of the couch and pointed her flashlight at the ceiling so that it lit the room with its dim glow. "The good news is that there's nothing wrong with the fuse box. The bad news is that all of the houses on the block are out—it looks like there's a power outage."

"Oh, no!" Ryan said in mock horror. "That means the fridge isn't working—we'll have to eat all of the ice cream in the freezer before it melts!"

There was a knock at the door. "Maybe after the pizza," Penny said. "Amanda, you know where the candles are, right? Why don't you light a few? It looks like we'll have to get used to the dark for a while."

I was bummed to have to let go of Dave's hand, but I didn't really have any choice. Penny and Felicia went to the front door to get the pizza while I searched the cabinet for candles and a box of matches. Dave helped me light them, and we spread them around the room. In a few minutes the living room was lit with a warm yellow glow. I turned off the flashlights and put them on the table, just in case we needed them later, while Penny handed out slices of pizza. It was just plain, but it was delicious. And somehow the warm candlelight made the house seem cozy and romantic instead of scary. We ate in silence for a while as the rain continued to fall gently against the window. Every now and again low thunder would rumble and there would be dim flashes of light outside the window, but it seemed like the worst of the storm had passed.

"We should have dinner by candlelight more often," I said. "This is fun!"

It was as if my words had broken a spell because the minute I spoke, the lights came back on. I blinked as my eyes got used to the light.

"Bummer," Ryan said. "I was really looking forward to eating that ice cream."

"Oh, well." Dave glanced at his watch. "My dad is coming to pick me up in a few minutes, anyway."

"Same here," Felicia agreed.

"Do you guys need a ride?" Dave asked Ryan and Nandi.

"That would be great," Nandi said. She smiled at me and added, "I told my dad that I was at a student government meeting—which is kind of true. But I think he might get suspicious if he showed up here and saw all the musical instruments and everything."

"Good thinking," I told her, but secretly I was glad that I didn't have to tell my parents half-truths about what I was doing.

Everyone gathered their things, and soon the doorbell rang. It was Mr. Fiol.

"Luis!" Penny said when she threw open the door.

"Come in out of the rain for a second. Would you like some pizza?"

"Oh, no thanks," Mr. Fiol said. His dark eyes danced, and he was smiling at Penny. "I've already eaten." He put his umbrella into the stand by the door.

"Take a look at what the kids have been up to," Penny said as she handed him one of Dave's flyers. "Isn't this great? Felicia's a terrific flutist, by the way."

Mr. Fiol looked at Felicia and smiled. She blushed and looked at her shoes. "I'm very proud of what you're doing," Mr. Fiol said. "And that goes for all of you." Even I flushed a little under the praise. A compliment from Mr. Fiol meant a lot—he didn't give them often, but when he did, he meant it. He turned to Penny and added, "It's wonderful that the kids have someone like you to help them."

"Oh, no problemo," Penny said, waving her hand dismissively. "They're doing everything themselves, anyway. I've barely done anything."

"Dad, I think I'd better get home," Felicia said, looking at him uncomfortably. "I still have some homework to do."

Mr. Fiol frowned slightly. "What do you say to Penny?" he asked.

"Thanks, Penny," Felicia said.

"Oh, sure thing, sweetie. See you tomorrow." Penny reached out and gave Felicia a little hug. At first Felicia was kind of stiff, but finally she loosened up and hugged Penny back. "And I'll see you Friday night," Penny said to Mr. Fiol, giving him a peck on the cheek.

Mr. Fiol and Felicia pulled away just as Mr. McClintic pulled up. He dashed up the front walk and rang the doorbell. "I'm here for Dave," he said to Penny. "I'm Bob McClintic."

"Oh, nice to meet you," Penny said, and introduced herself.

"Dad, can we give Ryan and Nandi a ride home?" Dave asked. "They're on the way."

"Sure," Mr. McClintic said, pushing his glasses up onto his nose. His hair was slightly damp from the rain.

I watched from the front doorway as Nandi, Ryan, and Dave said good-bye and headed down the front walk. As they were piling into the McClintics' minivan, I heard Dave tell the others that he'd forgotten something. He rushed up the front walk.

"What did you forget?" I asked as he pulled me into the front hall.

"Oh—just this." Blushing, Dave gave me a quick kiss on the cheek. Then he turned and hurried out the door. It all happened so fast, I didn't even have time to react. I didn't even remember to wave as the minivan drove away into the dark and rainy night.

The phone rang just as I was pulling on my pajamas that night. I glanced at the clock. Ten-thirty. I wondered who was calling—it was kind of late for a school night. I ignored it, figuring the call had to be for my parents. Besides, it was against Kempner family rules to answer the phone after ten. But when I heard Arielle's voice speaking into the answering machine, I picked up the cordless and pressed talk. After all, my parents were out. And I knew that if Arielle was calling, it had to be important.

"Hello?" I said. "Arielle?"

"Hi." Arielle's voice was warm, but I hesitated, unsure what to say. *Why is she calling me?* I wondered. Arielle cleared her throat. "Listen, Amanda . . . I just wanted to say—um—good luck."

"Good luck?" I echoed, staring at the receiver. What was she talking about?

"Yeah, you know—with tomorrow. The presentation," Arielle explained. "Good luck or break a leg or whatever."

"Oh," I said. "Thanks." I sat down at my vanity table. There was a photo of Arielle stuck to the mirror. She wasn't smiling in the picture, just staring back at me with a steady, confident gaze. I wondered why she had finally decided to stop being mad at me. That was the thing about Arielle—it was almost impossible to predict what she was going to do. It could be a pain, but it was also one of the things that I loved most about her. "Thanks so much," I said warmly.

"You're welcome," Arielle said. "I just—uh—wanted you to know that even though I think the athletics department deserves the money from the budget, I totally support you. As a friend."

I smiled at the photo on my mirror. "I'm sorry, too," I said with a sigh. "I guess I kind of overreacted. I just don't want the arts classes to disappear, that's all."

"I know," Arielle replied.

There was a brief pause, and finally I had to ask, "So—does this mean that we're best friends again?"

"Forever," Arielle said firmly. That was just what I wanted to hear. "Okay, listen, my mom will give me a major lecture if she finds out I'm using the phone so late, so I'd better get off."

"Okay," I said. "Good night. And Arielle?"

"Yeah?" Arielle asked.

"Thanks for calling."

"Oh," she said. "Oh, sure. That's what friends are for, right? Well, good night, Amanda Panda."

I smiled at the nickname that Arielle had given me when we were in the first grade. "Good night," I said, and clicked off. I put the phone on my nightstand and crawled into bed. It was still raining outside, but it had slowed to a steady drizzle. I bet that it would be a sunny day tomorrow. And no matter what happened, after tomorrow my presentation to the school board would be over. For better or worse, that would be one less thing I had to worry about. I was surprised at how

100

calm I felt. I guessed it was because I knew that I had so many people supporting me: Dave, Felicia, Penny, Nandi, Ryan, and even Arielle. *If only things would get back to normal with Traci*, I thought, *then everything would be all right*. But I tried not to dwell on it. I would worry about it after my meeting with the school board. She probably needed some time to cool off, just as Arielle had.

I pulled the covers up to my neck and felt the place on my cheek where Dave had kissed me. I knew it was impossible, but it was still warm.

I dreamed about that kiss all night long.

chapter
ELEVEN

School Board Meeting Agenda, December 14

1. Budget reallocations and funding for extra-curricular programs
2. Possible disciplinary actions regarding recent vandalism of sixth-grade boys' rest rooms
3. Yearly boiler maintenance schedule
4. Approval of revised cafeteria menu, including new vegetable choices
5. Policy on staff reimbursement for purchase of school-related materials

"Hey, Dad," I said as I walked into the kitchen. Dad was seated at the yellow breakfast table. Jessy and Joey were there, too, eating sloppy hot dogs. I guessed Adele was stuck at work again. I decided to fix myself a sandwich. I had to head over to the school board meeting in a little while, and I didn't want to go on an empty stomach.

"Hey, Amanda," Dad said, giving me a grin. "Adele should be home in an hour—can't you wait for dinner?"

"I've got the school board meeting tonight at seven," I said, pulling open the fridge. I grabbed a loaf of bread and dropped two slices into the toaster. Then I pulled out some peanut butter and jelly. I had a serious case of stomach butterflies and didn't think they would tolerate anything complicated.

"Oh, right," Dad said as he wiped up some milk that Jessy had spilled. She gave me a big chocolate-milk grin as I sat down at the table next to her with my sandwich. "Do you need a ride to the meeting?" Dad asked.

I shook my head. "Penny's taking me," I told him. "But thanks." Just then the doorbell rang. "That's probably Felicia," I said as I carried my sandwich to the front door. I looked through the peephole. It was Felicia, all right, standing on the doorstep in a parka, shivering. "Come in," I said as I yanked the door open. An icy blast of air followed Felicia as she hustled inside.

"It's freezing out there!" Felicia said as she stepped into the front hall. Her cheeks were flushed bright pink from the cold.

When I looked outside, I noticed that a few tree branches still littered our front lawn—I guessed Dad would take care of them later, once Adele was home. That had been some storm the night before. It seemed to have brought the cold weather with it. "Come in and warm up," I said as I shut the door.

Felicia pushed back her hood and placed her flute

case on the hallway table. "I'm so excited," she said breathlessly. "Aren't you?"

"About the presentation?" I asked. The minute I said the word *presentation*, the butterflies in my stomach started having a field day. "Actually, I just can't wait for it to be over."

Felicia smiled at me, her dark eyes dancing. She knew that I hated public speaking. "You'll do great," she assured me. "Don't worry."

I tried to smile at her, wishing that I felt as confident as she looked. Felicia peeled off her parka and hung it on the coatrack in the hallway, then followed me into the living room. The minute we sat down on the couch, the phone rang. I grabbed the receiver.

"Hello?" I said.

"Hey, Amanda, it's Dave."

The minute I heard Dave's voice, a warm feeling spread through my chest and the butterflies settled down. "Hi," I said. I felt a huge smile wrap itself across my face. Felicia looked at me with lifted eyebrows. I mouthed, "It's Dave," and she nodded.

"I've got the painting and the black cloth," Dave said. "I just wanted to ask you if there was anything else I should bring to the meeting."

"I can't think of anything," I told him. "Just bring yourself."

"I think I'll remember *that*," Dave joked. "Okay, well—I guess I'll see you at seven, then."

"Okay," I said, smiling into the receiver, "see you."

We said good-bye and hung up.

"What?" I said when I saw Felicia. Her lips were pursed and her eyebrows lifted into a funny expression.

"You!" Felicia said, her face breaking into a grin. "You can't stop smiling!"

I giggled and my palms flew to my cheeks as I tried to press my face back into its normal form. But it was no use—Felicia was right. I just couldn't stop smiling!

"So?" Felicia said, leaning forward slightly. "Are you and Dave officially together?"

I bit my lip, hesitating. I knew that Felicia wouldn't press me, but I decided to tell her, anyway. I was too excited to keep it to myself! "Dave kissed me last night."

Felicia's dark eyes grew round. "Really?" she squealed.

"Just a peck on the cheek when nobody was looking," I admitted.

"Ohmigosh, I can't believe it!" Felicia said.

"Me either!" I said, giggling.

"I wonder if Ryan has admitted that he likes Traci yet," Felicia mused.

"Probably not," I said. "I mean, neither one of them is really the gushy type." The minute the words were out of my mouth, I felt a pang. Of course, I had no idea what was going on with Traci and Ryan. After all, Traci and I were hardly speaking. I was going to say something about it, but just then I heard a key rattle in the lock and the front door swung open. I figured it had to be Penny—she had her own keys to my house.

"Hi, girls!" Penny said when she saw us. She was wearing a long, straight gray skirt and a soft-looking pink sweater beneath her red coat, and her hair was tied into a neat bun at the base of her neck. I smiled. I'd only seen her dressed up once or twice before. Usually, she wore jeans and loose shirts—comfortable clothes. She looked very professional, but her face was flushed with excitement. "Ready to knock 'em dead?"

"As ready as I'll ever be," I griped, but—actually— I felt pretty good. Suddenly, I was eager to tell the school board what I knew. I was sure that they would be impressed with our presentation. And even if they didn't give us all of the funding we were asking for, I figured that we would at least get *some*.

"I can't wait," Felicia said as she hopped off the couch. "Let's go!"

I brought my half-eaten sandwich into the kitchen and kissed my dad and the twins good-bye. Then Felicia and I grabbed my notes and her flute and piled into Penny's car. Penny turned up the heat, but Felicia and I were still shivering as the car pulled onto the road.

"School board, here we come!" Penny sang.

"You'd better get ready!" Felicia added, giggling.

Penny gave the horn a playful tap, and I turned up the radio. We were finally on our way. And nothing was going to stop us now.

I spotted Dave, Traci, and Ms. McClintic heading toward the auditorium entrance as we pulled into the parking lot. I rolled down the window and shouted, "Hey!" waving like a maniac.

Dave turned and hurried over. He was carrying a large painting of a seascape. Ms. McClintic had a black cloth draped over her arm. Traci hung back, looking uncomfortable.

"Hi," Dave said, leaning over and peering into the car window. "I'm about to go set up. I'll save you guys seats, okay?"

"Sounds great," I told him. "Thanks!"

He gave me an extrawide smile before turning back to the entrance, and my heart lifted. But it sank a little again when I glanced over at Traci, who looked like she couldn't decide whether to follow Dave and her mom or come over and speak to us. "Penny," I said suddenly, "can Felicia and I wait for you at the entrance while you park the car?"

"Okeydokey," Penny said. "You guys go in and warm up—I'll be there in a sec."

Felicia and I scrambled out of the car just as Traci opened the entrance to the auditorium. "Traci!" I called, and she turned to face us, her eyebrows lifted in surprise. "Wait up!" Felicia and I hurried over, and we all walked into the front entranceway together. It was pleasantly warm inside after the chill of Penny's car. I stamped my feet, trying to get some feeling back into them.

"So," I said as I pulled off my orange-and-pink-striped scarf, "how's it going?"

"Oh," Traci said vaguely, "fine, I guess."

There was an awkward silence. For a moment I considered telling Traci about what had happened the night before with Dave, but I immediately rejected the idea. Something told me that Traci wouldn't think that the story was cute—she'd think it was disturbing. I had to find something else. "Uh—how's soccer going?" I asked, desperate to fill the void. I couldn't believe that I was having so much trouble talking to one of my best friends.

Traci's shoulders lifted quickly, then dipped. "It's okay," she said.

"Arielle says that you guys might have to practice in the gym for a while if it stays cold," Felicia put in. I could tell that she was as uncomfortable as I was.

"Hmmm," Traci said. "Is that true? I hadn't heard. I haven't really spoken to Arielle much lately." I studied her face as students and faculty streamed past us on their way to the school board meeting. I wondered whether Traci and Arielle were still giving each other the cold shoulder over the game they had played the week before. I guessed they probably were. Traci looked behind her, as if she were eager to escape from us into the noise of the rapidly filling auditorium.

"Okay, here I am," Penny said as she bustled toward us. I was embarrassed by how relieved I was to see her. I wasn't sure that I could stand another moment of awkwardness with Traci.

"I think Dave said he'd try to get seats at the back," Traci said as we walked into the auditorium together.

"There he is," Felicia said, pointing. Dave was waving at us from his seat. He was with Ms. McClintic, Nandi, and Ryan, and it looked like they had reserved us an entire row. Nandi was wearing a flowy skirt over a leotard, and Ryan had his violin in his lap.

Ryan was studying a piece of paper as I slid into the seat between him and Dave. "What's that?" I asked him as Felicia took the seat between Dave and Ms. McClintic and Traci sat between Ryan and Nandi.

"It's the meeting agenda," Ryan said. "I can't believe that they're actually thinking about taking disciplinary action over a couple of spitballs in the boys' room. I mean, I'm sure that whoever did that was only having some innocent fun. And I'm sure that he would have cleaned up the spitballs if he hadn't had to rush to science class—or, you know, wherever. . . ."

Traci rolled her eyes and shook her head as Ryan went on, "And I can't believe that the school board is actually going to discuss new vegetable choices when they can't even make a hamburger that isn't disgusting. I mean, where are their priorities?"

"You should lead a protest," Traci joked.

"Believe me," Ryan told her, "I will. Once this violin gets fired up, there's no stopping it," he said, gesturing to his violin case.

I laughed a little, glad that Ryan was here. It made being with Traci a little easier. Now that we were actually in the auditorium, my butterflies were back—full force. I scanned the crowd, trying to find supportive faces. I spotted Mr. Tate in the third row and felt a little better. But then I saw Asher and Cassandra walking up the aisle. Ugh. I'd almost forgotten that they were going to be speaking, too. Asher turned and saw me, and I had to fight the urge to hide under my chair. But he gave me a smile and a big thumbs-up, and I felt a little better. He might be there to support funding sports, but it was nice that he didn't feel he had to be *against* the arts. I gave him a thumbs-up back.

Felicia leaned over and tugged on my sleeve. "Hey," she whispered, "what's going on?" She jerked her head toward the stage, where a few of the members of the school board—a pudgy man with a comb over and two women—had taken their seats. They

110

were covering their microphones with their hands and were leaning together, whispering fiercely. The man shook his head, and one of the women was scowling at something the other woman was saying.

I didn't have a good feeling about this. "I don't know," I said.

"They look upset about something," Dave put in.

"Probably just a little debate about what kinds of vegetables are most disgusting," Ryan volunteered. "You know, so that they can be sure to put them on the menu."

I bit my lip, hoping that Ryan was right. Even though I knew in my heart that he wasn't.

chapter
TWELVE

The school board meeting started late. There was a good deal more whispering once the other two members arrived. Finally, the pudgy man, who seemed to be in charge, cleared his throat and spoke into his microphone. "Can everyone hear me?" he asked.

Everyone in the auditorium chorused, "Yes."

"Good," the man said. "My name is Verlon Childs, and I'm the chairman of the school board. First of all, I'd like to welcome you to this open meeting. I don't remember the last time we had such a turnout. Now, I'd like to turn everyone's attention to the agenda. As you see, we have quite a few topics to discuss, so I'd like to ask everyone to keep their comments brief and to the point."

I gulped, hoping that the school board would consider our presentation "brief." It took a couple of minutes, but I thought we had condensed our information pretty well.

"Now," Mr. Childs went on, "the first agenda item is budget allocations for extracurricular activities. Uh, yes?" Mr. Childs peered at me over his bifocals. I hadn't even realized that my hand had shot into the air. I stared at it a minute, surprised.

Dave elbowed me in the side, and I stood up. "Uh—yes, Mr. Chairman, uh, I have a few remarks I'd like to make. . . ." I heard a click as Felicia snapped open her flute case. "I'm Amanda Kempner, and I'm president of the sixth grade here at Wonder Lake Middle School. I'd like to say a few words in defense of the arts program," I went on, gathering steam. "I don't think it's fair to cut the funding." Nandi leaned forward, poised to pull herself out of her chair. The painting was set up at the back of the auditorium. The plan was that we would perform there. Sure, the audience would have to turn around in their seats to see us, but the school board would have an excellent view, and that was the most important thing.

Mr. Childs pressed his lips together and glanced at the other school board members. One of the women—the one who had been scowling earlier—shook her head. "I'm sorry," Mr. Childs said, "but I'm afraid that the funding is going to have to be cut. The question is merely by how much."

"But it isn't fair to fund sports and not arts—" I protested.

"We won't," Mr. Childs replied, shaking his head. "As you know, there was a terrible storm last night. It seems that a tree fell over and landed on the grounds-keeper's shed. It completely crushed the shed and all of the grounds equipment. We can't afford not to maintain the grounds and buildings, so money from extracurricular activities will have to be diverted to replace the lost equipment, not to mention removing the tree and rebuilding the shed. I'm afraid that we're going to have to cut money from both the arts *and* the sports budget, Amanda."

My mind was reeling. They were going to cut both budgets? This was the worst possible news. "By—by how much?" I asked weakly.

The scowling woman leaned toward her microphone. "We'll start with the supplies and equipment budgets," she said, "and if that's not enough . . . I'm afraid that we'll have to rethink the faculty and the programs as a whole."

I glanced at Nandi, whose brown eyes were wide with horror. I couldn't believe this. "But—but—" I stammered. Weren't we even going to get to perform our presentation?

"I'm afraid there's no alternative," Mr. Childs said. "We'll have to table this discussion until the next meeting, when we have a better idea how much the repairs will cost." His voice was firm but kind. I got the impression that he didn't like the situation any more than I did. But there was nothing that any of us could do about it.

That was it, then. No one would even see our presentation. We'd done all of that work for nothing.

I slumped back in my chair, my mouth clamped shut. Dave looked at me sympathetically, but I looked away. I couldn't look at him right now. I couldn't deal with anything. It was taking all of my willpower to keep myself from crying.

I couldn't believe that I'd gone through so much—including fights with my best friends—only to end up with less than zero.

"Well, that was fun," Ryan said as we slid into a booth at the Cultured Cow, a tiny ice-cream shop that served up delicious homemade flavors. Penny had suggested that we go out for a treat after the disastrous school board meeting. Believe me, we needed it. As I looked around the table, I could tell that everyone else was just as bummed as I was.

"I still can't believe it." I shook my head sadly.

"Tell me about it," Ryan agreed. "How could they have approved creamed spinach as a new lunch vegetable?" He shuddered.

"Ryan, be serious," Traci snapped. She was looking at her mom, whose mouth was clamped into a tight line. I knew that Ms. McClintic must be worrying about her job. Traci looked worried, too. Ryan opened his mouth to say something but shut it again when he saw the look on Traci's face. I felt bad for him. I knew he'd just been trying to make everyone feel better.

"Hey, cheer up," Dave said. "We gave it our best shot. And maybe the damage to the grounds isn't as bad as they think—maybe they won't need that much money."

I tried to smile at him. I knew he was just trying to help, but part of me was worried that the damage was *worse* than they thought and that the budget would have to be cut *more*.

"I just hope they don't cut *all* of the art classes," Nandi said quietly. She'd barely said a word all evening.

"Yes," Penny said, "Amanda told me that you're very talented." Penny looked thoughtful. Her blue eyes had turned a stormy gray, and I wondered what she was thinking.

"They can't cut them all," Felicia said nervously, "can they?" She put her chin in her hands miserably. If the school cut orchestra, there was no way that Felicia's parents could afford to pay for private flute lessons.

"I certainly hope not," Ms. McClintic said.

Traci bit her lip and frowned at the table.

I know there's a saying that misery loves company, but right then, I was feeling the exact opposite. The fact that my friends were bummed about the cuts to the arts program was just making me feel worse. Especially since there was nothing I could do about it.

The waitress came over and we all placed our orders. Ryan ordered the "Tasty Trough," which came with two bananas, five scoops of ice cream, five toppings, whipped cream, nuts, and a cherry.

"I'll split that with you," Dave offered.

"No way!" Ryan said. "I have to make up for all the ice cream I didn't get to eat last night when the power came back on."

I started to order my usual—a chocolate milk shake—then thought better of it. I remembered how good the white pizza had been when I tried it with Dave and decided to get something different. "I'll have a peppermint sundae," I said, "with hot fudge."

"That sounds good," Dave said. "Can I try some when it comes? I'll let you have a bite of my chocolate sundae with peanut butter sauce."

"Deal." I smiled at him, feeling a little better. After all, maybe we hadn't even performed our presentation—but we'd still had fun rehearsing it. And I'd gotten to know Nandi and Dave better, so it *hadn't* been for nothing. Besides, I was proud of myself for trying. Even though I'd been nervous, I'd stood up to the school board. "You know, the thing that I'm most bummed about is the fact that the school board didn't even get to see your comic," I said to Dave, who blushed—but he was smiling, too.

"Hear, hear," Ryan agreed. He pulled a few pamphlets from his backpack and handed them around.

"This is really well drawn, Dave," Ms. McClintic said.

"And it's so funny," Penny added. "It really gets the information across well. You did a great job on this."

"Amanda helped me with the writing," Dave said quickly. "She did a lot of the work."

I looked over at Traci, wondering what her response would be. I hoped that she wasn't totally weirded out that I had helped Dave with the comic. But Traci wasn't looking at me—she was staring at the pamphlet. She looked at it for a long time. I couldn't read her expression.

"I really wish they had seen this," Felicia said sadly. Silence fell over the table. I think no one knew what to say.

Luckily, the waitress came back with our ice cream, so we had a moment of distraction. "Mmm," Ryan said as he dug into his monstrous bowl of ice cream.

"Can I have a bite?" Traci asked.

"Mmm—oh, no," Ryan said, his mouth half full. "It's terrible." He shoveled another bite into his mouth. "You wouldn't want any of this; it's just horrible. Better let me take care of it."

Traci rolled her eyes and took a spoonful. "Wow," she said after a moment, "that's a lot of flavors."

"You athletes," Ryan said to her, "you never stop

eating."

Traci smiled and shook her head as she sipped her vanilla malt.

I took a bite of my sundae. It was delicious—the cool peppermint and warm chocolate were a perfect combination. I couldn't believe I'd never tried it before. "This is great," I said with a smile.

"See?" Ryan said as he picked the cherry off his enormous mound of ice cream. "Food brings people together. That's one way for you sports people to make money, at least."

"What is?" Traci asked.

"Sell food at the games, like I've been saying all along," Ryan said absently, taking another spoonful of chocolate sauce. "You could sell ice cream and pizza. Hey—maybe the orchestra can do that, too, you know—during intermission."

Traci sat up straight in her seat. "Wait a minute—say that again."

Ryan's eyebrows drew together in confusion. "During intermission?" he repeated.

Traci punched him lightly on the arm. "No, the whole thing."

"Sports teams should sell food at games," Ryan repeated.

"That's it!" Traci said. She looked at me, beaming.

"What's it?" I asked. Traci looked so happy that I almost felt guilty asking, but I simply had no idea what she was talking about.

"We'll have a benefit soccer game," Traci explained. "We've been itching for a rematch with Stanton, anyway. We can charge for tickets, and we'll have food—"

"And hot chocolate," Ryan put in.

"And the orchestra can perform at halftime," Ms. McClintic suggested.

"My mom could donate some stuff from the bakery," Felicia put in, her dark eyes dancing.

"Ohmigosh—this is such a great idea!" I cried. I dug around in my backpack and pulled out a little notebook. "Okay, let me get this down." Everyone started hurtling ideas at me, and I nearly got writer's cramp trying to catch up.

I heard the bell over the door jingle and looked up. Arielle had paused at the entrance, her forehead creased with a worried frown. I grinned and waved her over. "Arielle!"

Arielle hurried over. "Amanda, I came as soon as I got your message—" she began, but stopped when she saw everyone's smiles. Confusion flashed across Arielle's face. "But I thought you said it was bad news?"

"Grab a seat," I said, motioning to the empty place next to Felicia. "We've just come up with a plan." I explained what had happened at the school board meeting and our new plan to raise money.

"There's only one problem," Dave put in. "I thought the school board was afraid that selling food at games would create too much of a mess."

"Oh, you're right," I said, deflating a little. "I'd forgotten about that."

Arielle waved her hand dismissively. "I bet they'll reconsider it now," she said. "They really need the money. Besides," she added, looking at Nandi and me, "you guys are on the student council. Can't you organize a cleanup crew or something?"

"Write that down!" Nandi cried, but I was way ahead of her.

"And if this works, we can have another benefit to raise money for new uniforms," Arielle added.

"Yeah—you could challenge the school board to a soccer match," Ryan suggested.

"Oh, please!" I said with a laugh. "Who needs the school board?"

"That's right," Traci agreed. "We'll take care of this without their help!"

I grinned at her, and she grinned back. My head felt lighter, like a heavy weight had been lifted from my shoulders, and I couldn't stop smiling. Now we had a plan that I was sure would work. And it was all thanks to Traci.

I should have known all along that all I needed was a little help from my friends.

chapter
THIRTEEN

Stanton–Wonder Lake Rematch Menu!

Hot dog: $2.00
Slice of pizza: $2.00
Burger: $2.50
Turkey burger: $2.00
Veggie burger: $2.00
Fries: $1.50
Chips: $0.75
Cocoa: $1.50

Also available, courtesy of Fiol's Bakery:

Superhuge marshmallow treats: $1.50
Black-and-white chocolate-
chunk cookie: $1.50
Lemon square: $1.00
Chocoholic's Delight brownies: $1.00

All proceeds to benefit the Wonder Lake Arts
Program!

"Wow, look at all of this stuff!" Ryan said as he gaped at the menu for the Wonder Lake versus Stanton soccer rematch. "I can't decide what to eat first!" His Saint Bernard puppy, Lola, frisked at his heels as he placed his order at the concession stand.

I pulled my hat down over my ears and ordered a hot chocolate. It was a cold day, but the sky was perfectly clear. "It's a good day for soccer," I remarked.

"I can't believe we pulled this game together in less than a week," Felicia said, sipping her hot cocoa.

"Me either," I said. But everyone had cooperated, and the head of the school board had even called me personally to thank me for organizing the event. So far, it looked like it was going to be a big success— the bleachers were mobbed, and everyone seemed to be holding a drink or something to eat from the concession stand.

"Ew!" Felicia said suddenly. "Ryan, are you sure it's okay to feed a hot dog to a Saint Bernard?" Sure enough, Ryan had handed half of his hot dog to Lola, who was gobbling it up happily.

"Hey," Ryan said. "It's a dog-eat-dog world." He grinned at me, and I had to laugh. Ryan could be a little crazy, but I had to admit that on the whole, he was a really good guy.

"Let's go over and wish Traci and Arielle good luck," Felicia suggested.

"Good idea," I said. I slipped my hand into my

pocket, felt the two small boxes I had tucked away, and smiled. I couldn't wait to surprise Arielle and Traci with them.

Ryan and Lola trailed after us as Felicia and I walked over to the sidelines, where Traci and Arielle were warming up. Arielle was on the ground, stretching, and Traci was running in place nearby. They were both wearing intense frowns. I knew that they were anxious about the rematch—even though it was an extra game and didn't count toward the season's standings, I was sure that they wanted to play their best.

"Hey, guys!" I called. "We just wanted to say good luck."

"Came to cheer for us, eh?" Arielle said dryly, eyeing Ryan.

"No cheering this time," Ryan promised as Traci petted Lola. "I promise—clapping only."

Traci shrugged. "Go ahead and cheer all you want," she told him. "I'm getting pretty good at tuning you out."

"Oh, *really?*" Ryan asked, and they both laughed. "Listen, the stands are nearly full," Ryan said, glancing at the bleachers. "I'm going to go snag us some seats."

"Great idea," I told him. "We'll be there in a sec."

"Good luck, Traci," Ryan said as he tugged gently on Lola's leash. "You too, Arielle."

Once Ryan was out of earshot, Felicia turned to me and nodded.

"So, um—Felicia and I have a present for you guys," I said, pulling the two small white boxes out of my pocket. I handed one to Arielle and one to Traci.

"What's this?" Arielle asked as she opened the lid. "Oh, wow," she said when she saw the necklace inside. At the center was a funky Fimo bead shaped to look like a soccer ball. Arielle pulled it out and fastened it around her neck. "I love it!" she said, jumping up to hug me and Felicia.

"Penny helped us make them," Felicia said.

"You made them?" Arielle asked. "I can't believe it!"

I glanced over at Traci, who still hadn't said a word. "We were thinking about what you guys said about Stanton," I explained, "you know—that their new uniforms give them a competitive edge. So we thought maybe these would help balance things out for our side." Traci continued to stare down at the necklace wordlessly. I bit my lip. Didn't she like it?

"Well, this is absolutely great," Arielle said. "You guys are the best."

"Traci, Arielle!" Coach Talbot called suddenly. "Huddle up!"

"Be right there!" Arielle called back. "We'd better go," she said to me and Felicia. "But thanks so much—for everything. Let's go, Traci." Arielle waved to us and jogged off to join her team.

Traci looked up at me and squeaked out a strangled, "Thanks," before trotting after Arielle.

"Gosh," Felicia whispered, "do you think she liked it?"

"Yeah," I said. Traci had been facing me and not Felicia, so Felicia hadn't been able to see the tears in Traci's eyes as she said thank you. But I had. "I think she did."

We hurried to join Ryan in the stands. I grinned when I saw who was with him. Dave was eating a brownie and waving at us, and Patrick was in the seat next to him. The boys had saved us some good seats at the edge of the third row, and we slipped in past Ryan so that he could be on the end with Lola. I sat down between Felicia and Dave.

"Go, Traci!" Ryan shouted as the whistle blew and play started on the field. Traci's blond ponytail streamed behind her as she immediately stole the ball and dribbled it downfield. She passed the ball to Arielle.

"Let's go, Arielle!" I cried as she made a shot on goal, her French braid flying. It rocketed toward the net—and went in! Goal!

The bleachers erupted into cheers, and I think that our little section was loudest of all. Even Lola started barking like crazy.

"That was amazing!" Patrick cried.

"Way to go, Arielle!" Felicia shouted. "Super pass, Traci!"

I was clapping so hard that my palms hurt. "All right, Wonder Lake!"

Once we had settled down again, I felt a tug on my sleeve. "Amanda," said a voice.

I looked over. "Hey, Asher!" I said. He was standing at the end of the row.

"Looks like a big crowd," he said, eyeing the stands. "I hear we've already raised nearly two thousand dollars. And the concession stand is still open."

"You're kidding!" I said.

I looked over at Felicia, whose eyes were round. "Yes!" she cried, leaning over to give me a high five. A few more events like these and we'd be able to *expand* the arts budget—and the sports budget, too, of course!

"That's awesome!" Dave said. "Let's hear it for Amanda!"

"Well, it was Traci's idea," I said, his smile making me blush.

"Yeah, but you're the one who pulled it together at the last minute," Dave said. I couldn't help noticing that when he grinned, he got the cutest little dimple in his left cheek.

"I had a lot of help," I told him.

"That was a pretty cool shot Arielle just made," Asher went on, glancing toward the field. "She's a terrific player."

"She sure is," I agreed. Felicia shot me a knowing

look, and I grinned. Asher had once tried to set up Arielle with his cousin, but Arielle hadn't been all that interested. As I watched Asher smile in the direction of the soccer field, it occurred to me that I hadn't seen him hanging with his girlfriend much lately. I wondered whether the cute eighth grader was starting to develop a crush on Arielle himself.

Asher stayed and watched part of the game with us, then left to join his friends at the top of the bleachers at halftime. Ryan left to go to the concession stand and returned with another huge pile of food.

"Ryan!" I said. "Are you trying to wipe out the concession stand single-handedly?"

"Hey! I'm just doing my part to support the arts," Ryan protested.

"You should try a piece of my brownie, Amanda," Dave offered. "It's excellent."

I broke off a small chunk of his brownie and popped it into my mouth. The rich chocolate melted on my tongue. Delicious! "Felicia, your mom bakes the best stuff!" I said.

"Tell me about it," Felicia said with a proud smile.

When the second half started, Stanton tied it up right away. Suddenly, I was on the edge of my seat. Oh, no. What if Stanton pulled ahead? I didn't want our team to lose to them . . . again.

I could almost feel the tension running through the crowd like a fever. Suddenly, Ryan stood up and cupped his hands around his mouth. "Two, four, six, eight! Score before it gets too late!" he shouted.

"Ryan!" I cried.

He looked over at me guiltily. "Traci *said* that she could tune me out," he protested weakly, but he sat down again and contented himself with clapping and an occasional whoop.

But Ryan had a point. Out on the field, Traci seemed completely focused on the ball. She hadn't even glanced up at Ryan's cheer. Instead she was guarding her Stanton player as Arielle made a quick fake and stole the ball, then burst toward the goal.

Traci cut left and lost her player. She was completely open. Arielle could take a shot on the goal, but the goalie was watching her and a Stanton player was right on her heels. Arielle's head pivoted, and I knew that she had seen Traci. Arielle had only a split second to make her choice. . . .

Arielle pulled back her leg and sent the ball flying—straight at Traci. Without hesitating, Traci flew into the air and headed the ball into the goal. The goalie leaped for it and missed it by inches. A minute later the referee's whistle blew. The game was over—we had won!

The crowd went absolutely crazy! Dave reached over and gave me a huge hug, then pulled away, embarrassed, when he realized what he'd done. I didn't mind, though.

Felicia and I crawled past the guys and raced over to our friends. Arielle and Traci were hugging on the field, and Felicia and I wrapped our arms around them.

"That was great!" I said. "You guys were awesome!"

Arielle smiled at me, her green eyes dancing. I smiled back. I was proud of her for passing that ball—more proud than I would have been if she had made the goal. And I knew that she knew how I felt. Just then the entire Wonder Lake soccer team descended on us, patting Arielle and Traci on the back, shouting, and cheering.

I started to walk away, but Traci grabbed my elbow. "Amanda, can I talk to you for a minute?" she asked.

"Sure," I said, following her a few paces away from the wildly cheering soccer team.

"Traci—way to go!" some guy shouted from the sidelines.

"Thanks!" Traci said, waving. Then she turned to me, her face serious. "Listen, Amanda, I wanted to let you know how much I love this," she said, fingering the soccer necklace at her throat. "I just—I couldn't talk before. . . ."

"It's okay," I said, touching Traci's arm gently. "I'm glad you like it."

Traci heaved a relieved sigh, and we just stood there a moment in silence. But it was a good kind of silence . . . not like the awkward ones we'd had all week.

"I'm glad that Arielle passed you the ball," I said finally. "I know that you two can get on each other's nerves sometimes, but you really are a good team."

"Yeah," Traci said, nodding. She looked at Arielle, who was still being mobbed by the soccer team, then out into the stands. Ryan, Patrick, and Dave waved at her and cheered. She laughed and waved back. Her eyes seemed to linger on her brother a moment and then landed on me. "We're not the only ones who make a good team, you know," she said.

I blushed, knowing that she meant me and Dave. "Really?" I asked. I was so relieved that my head felt light—as if it might fly away like a balloon.

"Really," Traci said. "Look, I'm sorry that I've been kind of weird about . . . you and Dave. It's just— this has never happened before. . . ."

"I know it's kind of bizarre," I agreed. "And I'm sorry, too. I never should have discussed you with Dave. That was stupid. But—you're not the only one who's new to this. So . . . I just hope you can forgive me?"

"Of course I can," Traci said, leaning over to give me a hug. I hugged her back, thinking, *That makes two McClintic hugs in one day.*

It was the absolute perfect number.

chapter
FOURTEEN

Sign posted in the WLMS cafeteria:

Come one, come all to the dedication of our
new mural celebrating school spirit and diversity!

When: Thursday afternoon, 3:30 p.m.

To all those who have helped with this project,
a big, fat thank-you from your grateful art
teacher. To all those who didn't have time to
help—come to the dedication, anyway, and
see what a great job your classmates did!

"That's looking great, Dave!" I said as I took a step
backward. It was Tuesday afternoon, and we were finishing up the school spirit mural, which was going to
be dedicated to the school in a ceremony on
Thursday. I'd asked Dave to help since he was such a
good artist, and Felicia, Traci, Arielle, Patrick, Ryan,
and Nandi were there, too.

"I'm out of blue," Felicia announced, waving her

paintbrush in the air. She was standing on a ladder, and her breath came out in little puffs of steam. It wasn't really that cold, but we were all wearing jackets and hats, anyway.

"There's a new tub over there," Arielle said. She was pointing at a spot near my feet.

I grabbed the tub of paint and unscrewed the lid. "Here you go," I said as I handed it to Felicia.

"Thanks," Felicia said, dipping her paintbrush into the bold blue paint. "It's nice to have paint when you need it."

"Yeah—it even looks like you guys bought more than enough," Dave said, looking at the tubs of paint that were lined up at the foot of the mural.

"Well," Nandi said slyly, "we had a lot of funds from the soccer match." It had turned out that the repairs to the maintenance shed hadn't been as expensive as the school board had feared. Once the maintenance crew checked the equipment, they discovered that most of it was still in working order, so all that really needed to be repaired was the shed itself. We'd raised enough from the soccer game to fix the shed, and we'd even had a couple hundred dollars left over. More than enough for a mural. In fact, the fund-raiser had been so successful that the student council had agreed to organize a snack sale at all of the upcoming games, too, which meant that it looked like the sports teams would definitely get their uniforms. "We *may* even be planning another mural to go inside the cafeteria," Nandi added.

"Of course," I added, "you're all welcome to help out with that one, too."

"I'll be there," Traci promised. "This is fun!" She added some green to the tree she was painting, then stepped back and frowned.

Ryan saw her look and rubbed his chin. "Hmmm," he said as he looked at her tree. "Slightly reminiscent of Rembrandt's later works, with a slight dash of Picasso thrown in."

Traci gave him a playful swat on the arm. "I just want to make sure it's even!" she said.

"It's even," Patrick assured her. "The whole thing is looking really good."

I had to agree. The mural had started as a picture of a giant muskrat waving pom-poms under a bright blue sky, but Dave and Nandi had added some figures to the background—a soccer player, a girl playing the flute, a guy on a skateboard, and a kid reading a book under a tree. The words *Go, Muskrats!* were painted above the scene. Somehow it managed to convey what Wonder Lake Middle School was supposed to be about—people with different interests working together. I was impressed with how well it had turned out.

"Look at all of these worker bees!" Penny called. The afternoon sunlight caught her hair as she walked toward us, making her look like she was lit from within. She was wearing a brilliant orange cape and carrying a giant Tupperware container.

"What have you brought us?" I asked.

"Just a few of my famous oatmeal-raisin cookies," Penny said as she peeled the lid off the top. "I figured you guys deserved a little break."

"Oh, my favorite," Felicia said, stepping down from the small ladder she was standing on. "Thanks so much, Penny," she said as she took a cookie.

"You're welcome," Penny said. Everyone gathered around, munching cookies.

"Mmm," I said as I took a bite.

Arielle gave the cookie a tentative sniff before taking a bite. "These *are* good," Arielle said. She sounded kind of surprised. I knew that she didn't think much of Penny's cooking.

"Wow, I love that tree," Penny said as she surveyed the mural. "The leaves almost seem to be moving in the wind."

"Nandi painted that," I said quickly. Nandi twirled one of her braids around her finger and looked at the ground. I could see that she was smiling, though.

"Nandi?" a voice called.

Nandi looked up, surprise written on her face. I followed her gaze and saw a tall African-American man in a gray suit walking toward us. He was handsome in a stern way and had a long, straight nose and full lips that looked a lot like Nandi's.

"Dad!" Nandi said with a gasp. She looked at her watch. "Oh, no!" she cried. "Ballet practice! I completely forgot."

"What's going on here?" Mr. Spencer asked as he joined us. "Nandi—I thought you were going to meet me in front of the school."

"Sorry, Dad," Nandi said quickly. "We were just painting, and I lost track of time—" She cast a longing glance at the mural. I knew that she didn't want to stop painting and leave for ballet practice.

Mr. Spencer looked up at our mural. His eyebrows lifted slightly. I couldn't be sure, but I thought he looked surprised . . . and pretty impressed.

"Mr. Spencer," Penny said, "allow me to introduce myself. My name is Penny Zinsser, and I just wanted to tell you how talented I think your daughter is."

"Zinsser?" Mr. Spencer said, frowning. "Have I read your name in the paper? You're an artist, aren't you?"

"Yes," Penny said with a smile. "I've had a few shows in town. Anyway, I wanted to let you know that I would be more than happy to give Nandi painting lessons at half of my normal rate. She planned this entire mural and painted most of it, including that gorgeous tree in the background. . . ."

I held my breath as Mr. Spencer looked at the tree. *Please say yes*, I thought. I was squeezing the handle of my paintbrush so hard that my knuckles were turning white. I looked over at Nandi. Her eyes were round, and she was looking at her father eagerly.

Finally, Mr. Spencer let out a sigh. "I'm sorry, Ms. Zinsser," he said, "but I'm afraid I can't accept your offer, although it is very generous."

I felt a lump in my throat as I sneaked a sideways glance at Nandi. She looked seriously bummed.

Mr. Spencer shook his head and went on, "I'll be happy to pay your *full* rate. We can certainly afford the lessons. And I think that Nandi deserves them." He smiled down at his daughter, and I couldn't help thinking that he looked much handsomer when his face wasn't so stern. "I had no idea you were so talented," he said to Nandi.

"Oh, Daddy!" Nandi said. She wrapped her arms around her father in a massive hug.

Mr. Spencer laughed. "Okay, okay," he said, "but now we really have to get you to ballet, or else Mademoiselle Diamont will yell at me."

"Fine," Nandi said happily. "Can you guys finish up without me?" she asked.

"Sure," I said. "No problem."

Penny offered Mr. Spencer a cookie. He took one with a smile, and then he and Nandi turned to leave. But as they were walking away, Nandi glanced over her shoulder and gave me a huge grin and a thumbs-up. I smiled and waved.

"I feel like we did a good deed," Penny said as she put her arm around me.

"We've done a *few* good deeds," Felicia said, wrapping her arm around me from the other side. "Thanks to you, Amanda."

"Oh, please," I said. I could feel my cheeks burning.

"Group hug!" Traci cried, pulling the four of us into a tight knot.

Arielle smiled and joined us. She had a goofy grin on her face, which made me giggle. Dave came over and hugged us, too. Then Patrick. Suddenly, everyone was laughing and hugging.

"Pig pile!" Ryan cried. He ran up to hug us but ended up knocking us over. I screeched with laughter as we crashed to the ground.

"Way to ruin a moment, Ryan," Arielle said, but she was laughing, too.

"I just made it *more* memorable," Ryan protested.

"Oh, yes—it's just perfect," Traci said sarcastically. "I'm getting squished!"

"Me too!" Felicia said with a giggle. "Help!"

I laughed. As far as I was concerned, Ryan was right—the moment couldn't get any more perfect than it already was. The arts budget was fine, the sports teams were going to get their uniforms, and I was with my friends on a sunny day.

Things just don't get much better than that.

Wondergirls #4: *"And the Winner Is . . ."*
Amanda Kepner knows she'd make a great class president but if she runs, she may lose her friends. They're all mad at her and now it looks like one of them might run against her! Is there any way to win this contest?

Wondergirls #5: *Perfect Harmony*
Traci, Ryan, and Felicia are in Chicago for an orchestra competition—and some fun. On top of that, Traci's met a really cute guy. Only problem: Felicia and Ryan can't stand him. What should she do? Hang with her friends? Or with this new guy?

Wondergirls #6: *The Makeover*
When Arielle gives Felicia a makeover, shy, quiet Felicia becomes the most popular sixth grader in school. But what about the former most popular sixth grader? Well, Arielle's not going to give up her title that easily—not even for one of her friends!

Wondergirls #7: *Birthday Blues*
Felicia wants one thing for her birthday and she gets her best friends, Traci, Amanda, and Arielle, to help her come up with a plan to make her birthday wish come true. But some birthday wishes won't come true—no matter how hard you wish.

Wondergirls #8: *Growing Pains*
Amanda wants to save the school's art program. Arielle and Traci think that the money should be spent on new soccer uniforms. Felicia agrees with Amanda, but she doesn't want to fight with her other friends. Can the four friends find a way for everyone to win?